WINTER'S LEGACY

WINTER BLACK SERIES: SEASON TWO
BOOK NINE

MARY STONE

MARY
STONE
PUBLISHING

Copyright © 2025 by Mary Stone Publishing

All rights reserved.

No part of this book may be reproduced in any form or by any electronic or mechanical means, including information storage and retrieval systems, without written permission from the author, except for the use of brief quotations in a book review.

❦ Created with Vellum

For the readers who stood by Winter through every storm—and in doing so, stood by me.

You didn't just support a series.
You gave me the courage to keep writing.
You changed the course of my career.
*You changed **me**.*

Because you loved Winter, I got to write full time.
Thank you for being part of this journey.
Thank you for making it possible.

With all my heart,
Mary

DESCRIPTION

He tortured her husband. Now he wants her soul.

Private Investigator Winter Black has faced monsters before. But Erik Waller is something else entirely—a sadistic fanboy of her serial killer brother who's obsessed with proving he's the ultimate predator. He's already left her family scarred and bleeding. Now he's taken a boy.

Just like Justin once did.

But Erik isn't copying Winter's past. He's rewriting it, turning her memories into a blueprint for fresh horrors. And he wants her front and center for the grand finale.

As Winter races to untangle Erik's grisly game, the lines blur between justice and vengeance, survival and sacrifice. Because Erik doesn't just want to destroy her.

He wants to become her legacy. And to make her his.

Winter's Legacy, the breathtaking final installment of the Winter Black Season Two series, is a haunting, heart-pounding finale that will leave you gasping. One last case. One final choice. And only one way out.

1

Harlan Lessner cursed under his breath, shivering against the cold concrete floor. His tongue had glued itself to the roof of his mouth, and crusted sleep clung stubbornly to his lashes. When he wiped at his eyes, his fingers brushed something sticky at his eyebrow. He brought them down. Blood.

What the hell happened to me?

As he inspected his face for other wounds, flashes of memory hit like aftershocks. A hospital room. His wrists cuffed to a bed rail while a surgeon sutured the bullet wound in his right arm. The anesthetic had dulled the pain, but not enough. Each pull of the thread had threatened to upend his stomach.

I deserved every second of that pain, and I know it. Kidnapping an FBI agent. Torturing him. Mutilating him.

Glancing around, he tried to determine where he'd wound up after the hospital. The room he was in now had no nurse, no bed, no handcuffs. Just a cracked window high on the wall, held together with duct tape.

He shifted to a sitting position, cradling his right arm to his chest. The bullet wound hurt like hell, raw and angry.

Using his left hand for support, he got himself to standing and shuffled to the window.

The glass was smudged, but not enough to obscure the view. Thick trees stood tall and menacing in the glow of what was probably a porch light. Otherwise, the night was dark and quiet. But lacking any sign of civilization, including everyday functional devices, Harlan could only guess at the time.

I'm in a basement in bum-fucking nowhere in the middle of the night. My chances of making it out of here alive are slim to none.

The realization brought surprising relief.

Harlan's life had been over for a long time now, ever since an intoxicated driver ran down his baby girl, Quincy. In the years that followed, he'd fallen into a depression that never really let up. His wife left him, taking their son.

Police work had sustained him, but he'd managed to screw that up too. All because of a man named Erik Waller.

The maniac had shown up and offered Harlan a deal. The chance to get revenge on the people who killed his daughter and a shot at reclaiming something of Quincy's life. Harlan's ex-wife had stored Quincy's childhood possessions in a cardboard box in her attic. Erik had stolen that box but promised to give that all to Harlan in exchange for services rendered.

He convinced me to kidnap Special Agent Noah Dalton in the name of tormenting Noah's wife, Winter Black.

The chance to hold his baby girl's favorite stuffed toy one more time, to remember her and keep her close to him—even if only in memory—was irresistible. His life had been nothing but empty days of quiet rage since her death.

So Harlan did the awful things Erik demanded, just to be reunited with the last remnants of Quincy's life.

But Erik didn't return Quincy's memorabilia. Instead, he coerced Harlan to do something even more heinous.

Flashes of memory came to him. Holding a gun to Noah's head while Winter pleaded with him. Eve Taggart finally shooting Harlan in the arm.

Darnell Davenport rushing in.

Harlan rubbed his wrists, recalling the metallic bonds that had secured him to the gurney in the ambulance. He'd faked a heart attack and killed an officer in his escape attempt, and Erik had helped him flee the scene.

But as they ate drive-through hamburgers in a deserted city park that night, a look of disappointment crossed Erik's face. *"Too bad I can't give you back the box. You were supposed to kill Winter's husband in the hospital room, and that didn't happen."*

Never once, in fifteen years of police work, had Harlan lost his cool.

He lost it then.

Hearing that shithead give yet another excuse for keeping Quincy's belongings, Harlan pulled his personal weapon out without thinking. Only at the last moment did he sway his hand. If he killed Erik, the location of Quincy's box would be lost forever.

That was an outcome Harlan wouldn't risk. Instead, he shot Erik in the leg, just above the knee.

Just as Harlan was congratulating himself on giving Erik a taste of his own medicine, he caught sight of a muzzle—Erik lifting a gun toward him.

Harlan's memories went fully blank after that. But he understood now why there was blood above his eyebrow.

None of that matters now. Where did he take me and why?

Turning around, Harlan used the light coming in from the porch bulb to navigate the basement. The room was empty with a short flight of wooden stairs leading up to a closed door. A slender band of light shined from beneath the door.

Harlan crept up the stairs, listening for movement.

He gently tried the knob.

Locked, of course. Erik's probably out there sleeping...just waiting to kill me.

That meant Harlan had probably two or three hours of freedom to explore his predicament and find a way out.

The wooden steps and banister were built of timber, old but not rotten and rough on the edges. The boards had never been sanded or finished. He tested the railing and found it sturdy enough to bear his full weight. But a few well-placed kicks could probably break the handrail from the balusters.

And the noise will wake up Erik, and he'll come in here and shoot me, or stab me, or do something else.

But at least Harlan would have a weapon in his hand when he died. The thought gave him some small comfort.

Bracing his back against the wall, he put a foot on the banister and pushed. Flexing his leg a few times got it rocking slightly, but the brackets and bolts holding the handrail in place wouldn't budge.

He picked up on a clicking sound, like footsteps on wood flooring.

What sounded like a refrigerator door opened, then shut, then opened again. Whoever was up there grunted. The familiar crack of a beer or soda can opening made Harlan's mouth water. What he would give for even an ounce of liquid.

The footsteps retreated from the door at the top of the stairs. Shuffling and a sigh preceded the telltale watery sounds of someone urinating.

Knowing this was his best chance, Harlan shifted his position on the steps and pushed on the banister again and again. He kept it up, rocking the wooden beam with all his might until it pulled away from the wall with a loud *snap*.

Just as Harlan regripped the two-by-four beam to wrench

it from the final post, something behind the steps caught his eye.

He paused, trying to make out what was in the shadows. He crouched. A cardboard box was tucked underneath.

The tip of a tiny pink rabbit ear spilled over the top.

Tears sprang to Harlan's eyes as he reached in and slid the box out of its hiding place.

"Quincy…"

The taste of his daughter's name robbed the strength from his legs, and he crumpled beside the box, reaching for the bunny.

What would Quincy think of him if she knew the things he'd done? Did he even deserve to touch her possessions, the items she'd once held in her hands with love and joy?

He trembled so hard his heart ached. Unable to resist a moment longer, Harlan clutched the bunny before scooping up a yellow baby blanket that had been folded beside it and held that close too.

He pressed the soft fabric against his cheek. Even through the musty smell of the blanket, he recalled the fruity and flowery scent of Quincy's favorite shampoo, a mix of berries and lavender.

A sob caught in his throat, equal parts happiness and misery. Happiness because everything he remembered was right here—Quincy's drawings, her favorite dolls, a small kite they once made together out of t-shirt fabric coated in sealing wax.

He could hardly believe his ex-wife had kept that. And that the psychopath he'd gotten involved with had gone in and stolen it from her home, using it to taunt him.

Sniffling, he stuffed everything down and folded the flaps of the box. Lifting it with his good hand, he braced the weight on his leg and hip as he stood.

Erik had to be upstairs. Whatever he wanted, Harlan

would happily offer. As long as he could keep the box of Quincy's memories, he'd kill a hundred people, cut off a thousand fingers. Nothing mattered as much as having a little piece of his daughter back, and Harlan would never again let anyone take her tangible memories from him.

He relaxed against the wall, his injured arm hanging limply at his side, the fiery ache from the wound radiating from his shoulder to his elbow. Just as he exhaled, trying to breathe out some of the pain, a click sounded from the top of the stairs, and the door above opened.

Erik stood there, silhouetted against light spilling in from the house behind him, a gun hanging loosely in his grip. "I'll be damned." He flipped on an overhead light and sauntered down a few steps, aiming the gun at Harlan's face. Harlan recognized it as his own firearm.

Erik Waller was in his mid-twenties, tall with a slim build and floppy blond hair. His pale face was long and birdlike with an angular chin and big, dark eyes that light fell into like twin black holes.

Harlan couldn't stand the sight of him.

"You found your box of goodies. I'm so proud of you. How's the arm, bro?"

"Hurts like hell."

"Getting shot hurts." Erik looked pointedly at his own leg. "I don't recommend it."

Harlan set down his daughter's things and backed away from the box as Erik came forward. Stepping into the open area of the basement would give him more room to maneuver while protecting his injured arm. If he had to rush the man, he'd have the benefit of weight, years of police training, and an uninjured shoulder.

"What do you want, Erik?"

"What every man wants, of course. Money, fame, and a loving *waifu*." When he spoke, spittle pooled at the corners of his heavy lips. "What did you tell the cops about me? I need to know what they know. Start talking."

The gun tracked down to below Harlan's belt.

He tensed his legs, knowing he could probably rush Erik and take him down. But with his aim centered on Harlan's groin, that might mean taking a bullet in the leg, too close to the femoral artery.

Play along and see if you can get him to adjust his aim. The second that muzzle shifts, you move.

Erik scoffed. "I'm waiting, cheese dick. What'd you tell the Feds about me?"

Harlan glanced at the gun and reminded himself to pull his gaze back up. Watching an attacker's face was always better than watching their hands.

"Who shot you?" Erik stalked closer and grinned knowingly, still holding his aim on Harlan's crotch. "Was it Winter?"

Any talk of Winter seemed to please Erik, so Harlan refused to give him the satisfaction of any details. He shot a quick look at the box of Quincy's things, and fat tears surfaced, wobbling in each eye.

"Thank you." Harlan's voice cracked. He cleared his throat. "Thank you for leaving that here for me."

Erik's face pinched. "What the hell you thanking me for? Bro, just tell me what the Feds know."

"I didn't tell them anything. They cuffed me, had me stitched up, and tried to take me to a third location…I recognized you. How'd you get in?"

"Shit, same way I got into your mom's pants last night. Walked in the door and told them I owned the place. For real, bro, they only had one cop in the ambulance."

"Where are we?"

"Somewhere and nowhere all at the same time." Erik

studied him. "You really didn't say a word about me? Not to anyone?"

Harlan laughed, the sound almost genuine. "I wish I could say I had. All I remember is telling Davenport that I was sorry. And for him to tell Winter and Noah I was sorry."

"Man, you are the weakest of weak sauce." Erik pursed his full lips and mocked Harlan. "'Ooo, wittle me is so sowwy. Pwease don't hurt me, Mr. Powiceman.' You're the king of being beta bitchtastic if ever there was one. What'd that get you? Huh? What'd you get for letting them step all over your balls like that?"

Harlan stared down at the pink bunny's fuzzy face. He could almost imagine the toy smiling at him, as if some part of Quincy were still alive and still saw value in him, despite what he'd done. "If you were a father, you'd understand."

"Fathers suck. Trust me."

"Yours did, and that's why you're like this. That's why you hate everyone and everything." Harlan knew which of Erik's buttons to push too.

"You want to watch that mouth."

"That sounds like something your dad used to say to you." He knew for a fact that Erik's father had mostly ignored him. With his mother dead, he'd been given money instead of love. The result of that upbringing was terrifying, the man in front of him living proof.

"I said shut your hole."

The muzzle tracked upward from Harlan's crotch.

Harlan leaned right, feinting briefly before launching himself at Erik, slamming him into the banister. The collision drove Erik's injured left leg hard into the rough edge, and Harlan enjoyed a second of victory as Erik yelped, his leg twisting below the knee at an unnatural angle. Then a sound like fireworks exploded in Harlan's ear.

That was all it was for a moment—just a sound that pulsed and echoed in the tiny chamber—as he and Erik stumbled together.

The fireworks exploded twice more. Pain erupted in Harlan's gut both times, and he staggered back. His legs became pudding, and he collapsed on the stone floor. Roses of blood bloomed on his stomach. He lifted his hand, barely aware of the ache in his injured shoulder, and touched the wound.

Harlan's fingers came away sticky.

Laughing, Erik kicked the box of Quincy's things, and it skittered across the floor.

Harlan's heart broke. "Quincy!"

"You fucked around, and you found out what happens to the non-player characters. You think you're special?"

Harlan gazed at the silhouette of the cardboard box, everything in his heart aching to hold the little bunny and the fuzzy yellow blanket, bring them to his nose, rub them against his cheek.

Above him, Erik stood gloating and laughing. "Yo, you stupid NPC bitch. You know what I got planned for your precious box?" He turned his back and set his hands on his hips. "Light it up. Burn it to a crispy crisp."

The gun barked again, and pain exploded in Harlan's chest. His vision went blurry. He tried to reach for the bunny, just the one thing, but a thunder of shots rang out, freezing him in place as bullet after bullet pierced his flesh. Once, twice, and a third time, a fiery hammer slammed into his chest.

Blood flowed thick and hot from the holes in his body. He pressed weak hands over the wounds as blood pooled around them.

He thought of his children, the only markers of success

he'd achieved in his miserable, wasted life, and he closed his heavy eyes hoping, though doubting, Quincy would be on the other side of this nightmare, waiting to take his hand.

2

Winter Black-Dalton leaned against her Honda Pilot in a line of cars outside Austin-Bergstrom International. The rush and roar of planes overhead mixed with the bustle of travelers, their chatter, and rolling luggage.

A few feet away, Noah hugged his mother again and planted a kiss on top of her head. She was only a few inches shorter than him, which made her taller than ninety percent of all women, including Winter.

"Have a safe trip, Mama." Noah yanked the pull bar up from her rolling suitcase and held it out. "Call me when you get home."

Liv Alvarez cupped her son's cheek and smiled, wrinkling the skin around her eyes. "I can always stay for an extra few days. I really don't mind."

"I'm gonna be fine. Besides, you gotta get back to your job. You're out of PTO."

She picked some speck of lint off his sleeve. "To heck with all that. My son needs me."

"Your son still has ninety percent of his fingers and a

hundred percent of his wife to help him. I'll be fine. And your flight is in, like, two hours."

"It just doesn't feel right, leaving you two like this." Liv looked at Winter with a soft expression. "You've been through hell. You deserve some pampering."

Winter laughed, remembering all the delicious meals Liv had prepared while in town. "You gave us plenty. Thank you."

"But…" Noah's mom cleared her throat, and her gaze floated to his left hand, which he'd stuffed into his pants pocket. "You haven't even gotten the bandage off yet. Maybe I should just wait until you get your prosthetic."

"I'm not even sure I'm gonna get one." Noah rolled his eyes at the suggestion, as he'd done every time his mother or Winter or any doctor brought it up. "It's just a finger. The only important thing it ever did was hold my jewelry. This little guy will just have to pick up the slack." He took his hand from his pocket and did a few up-down calisthenics with his pinkie. "Exercising. One, two, three, four."

"You're being ridiculous and using humor to hide your pain. Don't try to fool your mother."

He lifted a dark brow with suspicion. "You doubt the power of my pinkie?"

Winter bit her lip and looked down at her dusty boots, feeling vaguely invisible. "Don't worry. I'll make sure he looks after himself."

"I appreciate that. But who's gonna look after you?"

Noah shoved his left hand back into his pocket. He never used to keep it there, but that seemed to be where it lived these days. The bruising on his face and neck had improved a lot, though yellow bags still clung under his eyes, and his nose was swollen. Considering what he'd been through—being hit by a car, kidnapped, drugged, and mutilated—he was recovering incredibly well.

"Oh, fine, you stubborn ox." Liv met Winter's eyes again. "Make sure he cleans the wound just like the doctor said."

Winter smiled and nodded, stepping forward to receive her own goodbye hug.

Liv leaned in toward her ear. "If he gives you a hard time, call me, and I'll set him right."

"I know." Winter gave her a final squeeze. She waited with the car while Noah wheeled Liv's bag inside.

Winter walked around to the driver's seat and slipped inside. Her phone pinged with a text from her best friend, Autumn Trent.

Hey girl! Is Noah doing any better?

Winter smiled at her phone, like she always did when Autumn checked in. *He seems totally fine. Like nothing happened. I'm worried.*

Autumn replied almost instantly. *Why are men?*

I think you mean *why are Marines?

Touché!

The car door popped open. As Noah slipped inside, Winter set her phone on the center console. "Do you think she'll actually get on the plane?"

Noah clicked on his seat belt. "It's out of my hands now. Which is a good thing, 'cause my grip ain't what it used to be."

She smiled for his sake. Noah had always had a strong affinity for gallows humor—again, Marines. But there'd been a strong uptick in morbid jokes lately. She wondered how many more finger puns he could possibly have left.

At least one more. Every damn time.

She merged into a slow line of cars and followed signs to the highway. It was mid-morning, no heavy traffic to worry about, and the sun was high enough in the sky that she could put up her visor and slip off her sunglasses. They drove without talking for a while, the radio playing softly.

Winter reached over and gave his arm a quick squeeze. "You doing okay?"

"Hmm?" Noah glanced at her. His dark-brown hair hung shaggy over his forehead, brushing his eyes. His beard had grown bushy on his heavy, square jaw too. "I'm good. Got everything in hand."

She stifled a sigh.

"How are you?"

"Don't try to flip the feelings questions on me. You haven't said much about how you've been since we got you back home. I know you wanted to be tough for your mom, but you really don't have to. It's okay not to be okay. You know that, right?"

"This coming from you?" He leaned over and gave her a swift peck on the cheek. "I dunno, darlin'. If you must know…I've just had this weird feeling lately like something's missing, but I can't put my finger on it."

"Hardy har har."

Noah chuckled, and that had to be enough. He was handling the loss in his own way, just as she handled things in hers. The truth was she still hadn't figured out how to melt the tension from her shoulders.

If or when the day came that Noah actually wanted to talk about what happened to him, she'd be there. Always.

"I have a present for you." She reached into her jacket pocket and took out a small velvet pouch.

Noah reached over with his right hand—the one that still had five fingers. "What is it?"

"Don't get excited. I got it back from Darnell yesterday. I wasn't sure if you'd want to get it resized or…?"

He opened the pouch, and his wedding ring fell into his palm—a simple band of Damascus steel, acid-etched to show a stylized tree line, like winter reflecting in water. She'd threaded it onto a platinum filigree chain so he could wear it around his neck, seeing as the finger it was made for wasn't around anymore.

Noah's eyes grew soft and misty, just as they had the first time she'd given him that ring.

"The chain was Grandpa Jack's. He caught me looking for chains online and gave me that one. I guess it belonged to my great-grandfather."

"I honestly thought I'd never see it again."

"I'm not going to let your wedding band rot in an evidence locker. I told Darnell I'd sneak in and burgle the place in the middle of the night if he didn't give it back."

"And he believed you?"

"He gave me the ring back." Winter flashed a guilty grin. "I love you so much."

"I know."

She scoffed. "Okay, Han Solo. I'm gonna slap you."

"I love you too." Noah laughed and grinned like the Cheshire Cat. "Actually, I'm obsessed with you. It's weird."

He put his arm over her shoulder and kissed her neck. Winter's insides were tingling in the most pleasant possible way when her phone rang in the dashboard mount.

"It's Eve." She angled the screen toward Noah and accepted the call.

"Hey, Taggart. What's up?"

"Dalton? I didn't know they let you out at this time of day. Where's Winter?" Eve's voice was still a bit scratchy. Yet another aftereffect of Harlan Lessner's attempt to murder Noah in the hospital. He'd nearly strangled Eve to death—bashing her head against the floor multiple times to speed up the process—before he pulled a gun on Noah just as Winter barreled in and stopped him.

Keeping one hand on the steering wheel, Winter waved her free hand in front of the phone camera. "I'm here, Eve."

"Great. Swing by my office."

"Now?"

"I mean, unless you don't want me to tell you everything I've learned about Erik Waller since we talked three days ago."

"Erik who now?"

Eve snorted. "Erik Saulson's real last name is Waller. Really for real, not just another alias. Now, are you going to come talk to me or not?"

"Already headed in your direction, babe."

"Grab me a coffee?"

"Done." Winter hung up and bit her lip. "I can't help thinking Erik must have a stronger connection to Justin than just being one of his useless fans."

Noah furrowed his brow. "Why do you say that?"

"I talked to Autumn about him last night while you were asleep."

"Oh, yeah?"

"We ended up talking about that guy on death row who's become so internet famous with all the women lusting over him."

Noah's head fell back against the headrest hard, as if disgust and disappointment in general humanity had broken every bone in his neck. "Lord have mercy. It's *Beauty and the Beast*."

"What?"

"*Beauty and the Beast*. Women who feel threatened by men, whether subconsciously or not, can think monsters are sexy."

"I wonder what Autumn would think of your theory."

"I'm sure she'll be happy to tear it apart and explain why I don't know what I'm talking about. What else did Autumn say about Erik?"

Winter flipped down the visor as their path of travel put them facing the sun. "She said a lot of men engage in hero worship, even and often especially if the hero is violent. Such men choose cruel and violent individuals as idols because that was how their first idol, their father, behaved toward them."

"She's thinking Erik carries around resentment and has misogynistic tendencies because his father was abusive and his mother wasn't around to give him love and affection."

"Pretty much."

"It's always the parents' fault, eh? Makes you wonder why anybody ever has kids."

Winter grunted her agreement. "Erik might look at Justin, and maybe others like him, as a surrogate father figure…one that gives him permission to act on the violent impulses society has told him to resist and keep buried his whole life."

"I wonder if Justin and Erik ever met each other. Not just online, but in person."

She shrugged, but only to suppress a shiver. She could easily find out the answer to that question. The idea had been nagging at her like an earworm. Until Erik was behind bars, neither she nor her husband would be able to fully relax and recover from what he'd already put them through. Every moment he was free, they were in danger, as were all his future victims.

Winter needed to catch him fast, and she was willing to do whatever it took. Even if that meant making herself vulnerable to an even more hideous monster.

3

When they arrived at FBI headquarters, Winter and Noah went through security and headed straight for the office he used to share with Eve and her enigmatic bamboo plants, Pokey and Pokette.

Winter hugged Eve hard before handing the coffee over and taking a chair in front of her desk. Noah settled into his old spot and did a little spin in his office chair.

Does he miss the FBI? Does he regret taking time away?

Before Winter could go down that rabbit hole, she focused on Eve, who was looking a bit worse for wear, with an ugly ring of bruises circling her neck. Her hair covered a patch of five stitches, but Winter knew her friend was sore.

Lessner did that.

They'd only been friends for a short time, yet the thought of losing Eve for any reason already stabbed at Winter like fishhooks burrowing into her heart.

"How are you holding up?" Winter bit the corner of her lip before she remembered Lessner's punch had left a cut. She winced, absently stroking the matching bruises on her own neck as she took inventory of her recent injuries.

"Meh. Nothing that won't heal." Eve flashed a smile, but the moment of levity vanished almost as quickly as it arrived. She frowned and cast a glance in Noah's direction. "Sorry. I didn't mean…"

"Forget it." He wiggled his four remaining fingers at her. "I'm trying to."

Nodding, she took a quick sip of her fresh, hot coffee and turned her laptop around so they could both see. "Erik Waller's high school yearbook photo. Senior year."

On the screen, beside a drawing from a sketch artist, a face stared back at Winter. This was the first time she'd seen her stalker. Erik looked oddly harmless, with his long nose and nerdy smile, dressed in a pale-blue button-down and a sports coat. Winter had to read the name under the picture twice. "Is that really him?"

"It's him." Noah wagged a finger at the screen. "He had a beard, and his hair was brown when I saw him at the park that day, but I recognize those eyes and that smile. Like the middle of his mouth is numb."

"See now, I've never heard that story directly from you." Eve folded her arms and leaned back in her chair. "What was your interaction with him?"

"Nothing really. I didn't know who he was, of course."

"Of course."

"I was minding my own business when I noticed a scared-looking kid by himself sitting on a bench. When I went over to talk to him, Erik showed up and said his mom was searching for him. We waited 'til she showed up. That was it."

Winter's jaw hardened. She still couldn't believe how easily they'd been played. "It was a setup, of course. To take the pictures of Noah to send to me after he was kidnapped. To get close enough to him to prove that none of our security measures meant anything." She clenched her hands into fists. "It's all ego with someone like Erik. I'd bet my eyes the kid and the mom were plants."

"If you're gonna bet with body parts, use mine." Noah waggled his left hand. "Precedent."

Winter glowered at her husband before turning the scowl toward Eve when she let out a little chuckle. "Do not encourage him." She tried for a warning tone, but in seconds, the three of them were sharing a morbid laugh.

"Do you think he was wearing a wig?" Eve finally asked. "His driver's license has him as a natural blond. And blond again on your office security footage, but dark-haired when your assistant saw him at the office."

Flipping the computer back around, Eve leafed through papers spread haphazardly over her desk until she found a color photocopy of a Texas driver's license. "Last renewed when he turned eighteen. He's twenty-two now. Six feet, a hundred and sixty pounds."

Eve passed the page to Winter.

Once again, the man in the picture looked nothing like the monster living in Winter's head. Though, given everything Erik Saulson—no, *Waller*—had done, the only image of him that wouldn't give her cognitive dissonance would be if he were painted red and sporting a pair of goat horns.

Winter let out a deep sigh. "He's not even bothering to disguise himself."

"His ego's the size of Jupiter." Eve scoffed. "Which is awesome. It means his pride has him out there making dozens of mistakes. He's probably already made the one that'll lead to his capture."

Noah's phone buzzed. He pulled it from his pocket and narrowed his gaze at the screen. "It's my mom. Just a second." Standing, he excused himself and stepped into the hall, closing the door behind him.

Eve flicked her finger over the touchscreen of her laptop, her gaze roving back and forth. "Erik Waller was born in Onalaska, Wisconsin. At age eighteen, he moved to Chicago, where he attended the University of Illinois and studied digital media. He dropped out last November, a month shy of his bachelor's."

"That's weird. Why'd he drop out?"

Eve bit the corner of her bottom lip, her blue eyes focused on the screen. "His father was murdered."

"What?" Winter leaned so far forward in her seat that her backside hovered. "Was he a suspect?"

"He was questioned, but an alibi confirmed he was miles away from the scene."

Winter waved a hand dismissively as if being assaulted by a particularly annoying fly. "Proves nothing. Erik's favorite trick is getting other people to kill for him."

"Fair enough. Benjamin Waller was the head of an American video game company called Yorobo. They focused on console gaming and had recently put out a game that was really popular. Erik's father was successful, well known in his industry, and very rich. His murder made headlines across the country and internationally."

"How was he killed?"

"His body was found in his own bed with multiple stab wounds in the chest. Minimal defensive wounds, so whoever did it landed the first blow while he was still asleep."

"It could've been what started Erik down this path. The loss of the second parent. Or he could've killed his own father." Winter pressed two fingers to her forehead and raked them back. "Why not?"

After some serious rummaging in a creaky metal cabinet, Eve pulled up a brown file folder and tossed it across the desk—a cold case file of the unsolved homicide of Benjamin Waller. "I left a message this morning for the lead detective who worked the case out in Wisconsin. Hopefully, he calls me back soon."

Winter nodded as she flicked through the pages in the file, which included crime scene photos of a middle-aged man splayed out on the bed with at least a dozen stab wounds in his chest and stomach. He was dressed in pajamas, the duvet still pulled over the bottoms of his legs.

In her years on the job, and unfortunately even in the years before, Winter had been exposed to more gore than the human mind could comfortably comprehend. Nowadays, what made her most uncomfortable was recognizing just how little such images affected her.

The last person to see Benjamin Waller alive was one of his coworkers, who had a video call with him between nine and nine thirty on a Saturday night. The body was discovered the following Tuesday morning by his housekeeper. By the time law enforcement arrived on the scene, the body was completely limp. Based on rate of decomposition and other factors, the medical examiner of La Crosse County put the time of death between eight o'clock Saturday night and six o'clock Sunday morning.

Winter kept flipping pages, taking in the information. It was an unspoken rule that Eve shouldn't be letting her look at the case file, which meant she ought to assume she'd never get to look at it again after this moment. She wanted to milk the opportunity for all it was worth.

At last, she came to information regarding the victim's next of kin—his only son, Erik Waller. His initial police interview was summarized in the file. Erik claimed he was in school down in Chicago, hundreds of miles away from the scene. The story had been corroborated by his housemate, Joshua Sutherland.

Winter snatched a pen from a crude ceramic holder on the corner of Eve's desk with the words *Best Mom Ever* written on the side in green paint. She took a yellow sticky note and scrawled down Sutherland's contact information.

The door creaked as Noah stepped back inside—eyes narrowed and face paler than before. A little vein pulsed in his neck. He was more than simply irritated. He was absolutely furious, holding in a barrage of swear words with sheer force of will. Winter knew that face.

Her stomach clenched. Nothing trivial ever made that vein pulse. "What's wrong?"

"Can I borrow your credit card?"

"Sure." Winter went into her bag to fish it out. "Why? What's wrong?"

"Problem with my mom's ticket."

She removed the card from the leather holder and held it out between two fingers. "I remember the two of you arguing over who got to pay for it."

"I'm paying for it. But apparently my card has been declined or some crap." Noah snarled, snatching the card. "I'll call the bank after this." He put the phone to his ear again as he left the office. "Okay. Are you ready for the number?"

Winter stared at the pattern of his green-blue plaid shirt as he stomped back into the hall. A stone of dread dropped into her stomach.

"Everything okay?" Eve squeezed Winter's shoulder.

Winter's eye twitched. "You remember the little package Erik sent me the other day?"

"The one that gave us his fingerprint and led me to all the information I just finished briefing you on?" Eve shrugged. "Not ringing any bells."

Winter desperately wished she could laugh at the deadpan expression on Eve's face, but humor was smothered by her evolving thoughts.

"Well, dog tags." Winter rubbed her temples.

"Ah, right, his social security number."

"Right, but we notified the bank and our credit card companies. But something slipped through the cracks. Erik might not be spending our hard-earned cash, but maybe he's out there trying to cancel us out of existence."

"Maybe the bank or credit card company stopped payment on the flight. That would make sense."

From the hall, Noah let out a yell. "Son of a bitch!"

4

After finishing their chat with Eve, Winter and Noah headed out from headquarters. He barely said a word as they got in the vehicle, Winter at the wheel, driving in silence.

Noah finally called the credit card company to tell them it was him trying to make a purchase.

"Son of a bitch." Noah punched the ceiling of the Honda again. "A new card's in the mail. Whatever that means. Lotta good it does me right now."

Winter fought back a flinch. She hated when anyone got angry enough to hit things, having been on the receiving end of male anger one too many times. Conceptually, she knew she never had anything to fear from Noah no matter how angry he got, but her sympathetic nervous system didn't know that.

"I have my business card. We can keep using that until you get the new one." Winter forced her voice to stay cool and even. "And the Visa I had before we got married is still open. I haven't used it in a long time, but there's like a ten-thousand-dollar limit." She wanted to tell him that these extra precautionary measures by the company were a good thing. But his ego had been bruised when the purchase for his mom's flight hadn't gone through, with Liv only finding out when she went to check in. She understood that.

Noah frowned out the window. "Can't believe they can't just reactivate the card."

"If someone knows enough to be able to deactivate the card, they know the card number."

They both carefully avoided saying that *someone* was probably *Erik*.

When they pulled into the driveway at Winter's grandparents' house, he didn't leave the vehicle. Winter gave him a quick squeeze on his shoulder and went inside.

Dropping her keys in a bowl near the door, she inhaled the scent of beef stew simmering on the stove. "Gramma? Grampa?"

No answer came. Sudden and intense anxiety nipped at the back of her neck. Erik Waller was still out there, still obsessed with her for whatever reason. Of course he knew who her grandparents were and where they lived. He'd also made it clear he had no problem dragging her family into the situation, going as far as to murder her estranged father's sister, Opal, just to prove the point.

Stepping into the kitchen, she heaved a great sigh of relief when she spotted a note on the fridge. Her grandparents had gone out for the afternoon and would be home in time for dinner at six o'clock sharp.

Winter glanced at the cuckoo clock on the wall, which read a quarter past two. Her shoulders slumped as she took a seat at the breakfast table and grabbed a banana from the neatly appointed fruit bowl.

She and Noah had been spending a lot of time over at her grandparents' house to keep them safe. She wanted to be close to the people she loved because she knew in her bones that nothing lasted forever.

Any moment spent together could easily be the last.

Her heart pinched, and Winter recoiled from the explosion of doubt and insecurity. She couldn't allow herself to get into a dark or fatalistic place—only her all-encompassing, pigheaded confidence in her own abilities could ever hope to see them through.

At this point, they'd found so many cameras and microphones around her house and office, she didn't feel safe at either location anymore. Even though they'd checked and checked both, Waller had still managed to slip more bugs into what were supposed to be their safe spaces. Taking a shower in her own bathroom had nearly sent her into a panic attack, worrying that Erik somehow installed a tiny camera in the showerhead.

He never would've had a chance to do the same at her grandparents' house. They were almost always home, and the neighborhood consisted of a bunch of old busybodies who constantly minded one another's business. She'd only found one camera under the overhang of their back porch—her first tip-off that she was being watched.

Not exactly a selling point.

Another thought occurred to her as she took a bite of banana.

Erik Waller could have one of the neighbors in his pocket already.

She took out the sticky note she'd scribbled in Eve's office. Joshua Sutherland's phone number and address in Chicago—Erik's alibi for the night his father was murdered. Opening a browser on her phone, she started off by googling his name. When that brought up more results than she could handle, she opened Tracers and looked him up by entering all the information she had.

Joshua Sutherland was twenty-two years old, same as Erik Waller. Born in Aurora, Illinois, he attended the

University of Chicago where he graduated from the Department of Visual Arts.

After scanning and saving all the dry facts about the man she could gather, she switched gears and searched for him on social media platforms. She was alarmed by how quickly she found him and soon discovered that Sutherland had a rather extensive following.

She only had to watch about six seconds of one TikTok to understand why. With good looks and charm that vaguely reminded her of Harry Styles, Sutherland offered advice for fledgling artists. On his channel, he gushed about honest artistic expression and was always interviewing and showing off some other peers' work, which appealed to a lot of people, especially creative types.

Combing back through his profile, Winter spit out a bite of banana, just catching it in the peel.

Joshua Sutherland had recently taken a job at the Center for Fine Arts in Dallas. That was only a three-hour drive from Austin in decent traffic.

It could just be a happy coincidence, though Winter didn't really believe in those. What were the chances that Erik Waller and his old alibi would both independently move to Texas within a few months of one another? More likely, they were still connected. Could she be looking at yet another minion?

Winter glanced at the cuckoo clock, considering whether to skip dinner with her grandparents. A few minutes after two thirty. If she left now, she could be in Dallas by dinnertime.

5

I took a knee beside a beat-up Ford Escort and watched my new favorite person go about his closing routine at the little market where he worked. Streetlamps blinked in their frosty plastic casings above me, cheap light bulbs unchanged by underpaid city workers.

Thistles and dandelions grew in the cracks of the crumbling asphalt, but my jeans were thick, protecting me from the prickles. I rested a hand on a stack of old pallets at my side for stability.

The kid would finish soon, as he had every night since I started hunting him. First, he'd lock the glass public-facing doors. Then he'd do a bit of restocking and swipe a few things for himself, thieving bastard that he was.

Then he'd count out the till. Load up the day's take in a sealed plastic envelope, which he'd then drop in the bank's drive-through on his way home.

Except tonight, Manoj Bakshi wouldn't be making it home.

I had quite a few opportunities to get the jump on him, particularly since he wore headphones through his whole closing process. The trouble was the little mom-and-pop market was fitted with security cameras. Their range covered the entire store and the front lot. Not that I really gave a crap if I was caught on camera.

Nobody knew what I really looked like, since I always wore a wig and extra layers of clothing when I went out "for business." And when I did show my face and real hair to someone, they were pretty close to getting dead anyway, like that shit-bird Lessner I killed last night.

Harlan Lessner was the stinkiest, soggiest hunk of human garbage I'd met in my entire life. But unlike every other stupid chump I ever got to do evil for me, he'd actually managed to bite back by shooting me.

Even though Harlan grazed my leg with a bullet, I hadn't really wanted to kill him, seeing as how incredibly useful he'd been to my cause. But he gave me no choice in the end. Shit-talking about my dad was the worst mistake he'd ever made, and now I needed a new lackey to help me do my dirty work.

Unfortunately, being a serial killer didn't provide me an easy means of hiring an assistant. Couldn't exactly post the position on Indeed.

I also forgot just how much leaning and crouching was required when getting up to nefarious shit out in a public place, even in an abandoned parking lot. My leg was sore as hell.

That same night, just after stuffing the wound with scraps from old t-shirts and wrapping it in layers of duct tape, I found a site I thought I could trust and ordered some designer drugs—anti-inflammatories, anticonvulsants, antidepressants, psychedelics, and all the rest of that good shit no doctor would ever give me. One hour later, a box of pills was delivered by a cute girl with a pizza magnet on top of her car.

Money made the world go round. Facts. The only lesson my old man ever taught me.

After popping a handful of rainbow pills, I told myself not to focus on the pain, that I'd be fit in no time.

Winter.

My girl didn't know it yet, but everything in her world was about to change. The life she'd built for herself would end, and a new one would grow in its place. I was the gardener. I planted the seeds. Harvest time was coming.

With this in mind, I went over to Manoj's shitty little car, opened the door with the key I'd stolen last week, and made myself comfortable in the back seat. My little grocery worker had a spare key, of course. I was sure he figured he'd misplaced it and gave it no more thought. People made up their own explanations for strange happenings and inconsistencies in their lives, which made everything easier for wicked, underhanded bastards like me.

"Fuck it." I smiled, baring all my teeth. "We ball." The pink pill was gradually making everything less painful. That one was my favorite.

My boy would never notice me in a million years. Never once had I seen him check the back seat. He usually didn't even take off his headphones. I pulled up my hood and waited.

People who were unaware made the best victims.

I rubbed my injured thigh absently. The last thing I needed was another wannabe alpha dog like Harlan Lessner trying to butt heads with me. Better someone like Manoj Bakshi who I'd never once seen stand up straight. Never. Once.

And I'd installed a Wi-Fi camera outside his house, to keep an eye on his comings and goings. He was so scared he might accidentally look someone in the eye, he kept his gaze on his shoes all day long.

Poor guy didn't have a single alpha bone in his body, let alone the material to be a true sigma like me. He was pure beta. Not unlike women, beta males existed only to be dominated and forced into menial labor. It was time Manoj found that out and accepted his place in this pecking order.

The crunch of feet on gravel was followed by the rustle of the garbage bag in his hand. He went to the dumpster and pitched it in. The driver's door popped open, and he tossed his backpack and the bank deposit envelope onto the passenger seat before slipping behind the wheel.

Manoj gave a sigh so labored it sounded like it should've come from a ninety-year-old, not a nineteen-year-old. Then he put both his hands over his face and leaned into them to take a few breaths with slumped shoulders.

The backpack had sounded quite heavy when it hit the passenger seat, which made me grin. The most interesting thing I'd learned about Manoj—what cinched it for me—was his thieving. Food, mostly. I was pretty sure his family was poor AF.

But it wasn't a noble Valjean situation, as I'd seen him take other things as well. Things nobody actually needed, but he clearly thought might improve his pathetic life—acne medication, teeth-whitening kits, and the ever-hopeful pack of condoms.

I knew his bosses didn't suspect a thing because I'd gone into Black Cherry every other night for weeks now. That was where I got my dinner—feta cheese, tiny cucumbers, kibbe, and sour cherry juice. They had two small tables and chairs near the deli where I could sit and eat and listen to the drama.

The owners—a middle-aged Iranian couple—were having marriage problems, and Manoj had a crush on his boss's daughter, who was around his age and also worked at the store. She was kind of fine, I guessed, though she was hijabi, so it was hard to tell. She didn't like him, though. I overheard her tell her friend she thought Manoj was weird. One time, she even said he gave off serial killer vibes.

I laughed out loud when she said that. I had to agree. The kid had potential. Lurking somewhere in all his introversion and awkwardness, masked by a compulsive need to be polite, Manoj had a lot of resentment and anger. Clearly, he wanted to be a very different kind of person than he currently was. I was banking on that, actually.

If anybody could bring out the latent serial killer in a man, it was me.

Maybe this time I'd found a worthy protégé—one that would outshine Justin Black and his pathetic conception of what an apprentice should be. I mean, first there was the old man who looked at Justin like some kind of diabolical second coming.

Finally, there was the traumatized little redneck boy Justin took with him on his European vacation—the one he'd forced to participate in more than a dozen of the snuffiest torture porn videos on the dark web. Justin even dressed up the prepubescent boy as a girl and made him cosplay as his woman when he didn't want to sleep alone.

After beginning my own search for a decent apprentice or group of followers two years ago, I had to admit it was harder than expected. I'd had such hopes for Cybil Kerie. It really was unfortunate she was such a self-absorbed, backstabbing bitch. And Harlan Lessner. Well, Lessner. I wished I could bring him back to life just so I could kill him again.

Manoj mumbled to himself in a language I didn't understand or even know the name of. Then he started the engine and pulled out into the gathering night.

My little pink pill was taking full effect now. My leg didn't hurt anymore. Or maybe it did, and I just didn't give a shit. I fingered the gun in the big front pocket of my hoodie—the same Glock 22 I used to finish Lessner.

I usually preferred untraceable plastic when it came to firearms, but why the hell not? I'd never used a cop gun before. Feeling its weight and sleek coolness in my hands reminded me of Winter. I liked that—the power of it.

My baby was a warm gun. I could hardly wait to squeeze her trigger.

Having memorized Manoj's route home, I bided my time and counted the turns. First, he swung through the bank drive-through and deposited the envelope. Presumably to avoid stoplights, many of which lasted for minutes at a time, he drove home on an isolated road that ran along the perimeter of the neighborhood beside old railroad tracks and through an industrial area of town.

That was when I sat up and set the barrel of the gun against Manoj's temple. "I don't want you to panic. I need you to stay absolutely calm."

To my surprise, he didn't panic or freak out like a little bitch. His neck tightened, and his eyes bulged at my image in the rearview, but he replied in a voice that was both clear and uncharacteristically deep. "No problem, man. Whatever you want."

"Good boy. Now pull over and cut the engine."

Manoj nodded, and in a measured way that would make any driver's ed teacher proud, he eased the car to the side of the road and stopped. "Take the car. My money. Whatever you want."

I laughed. "Why the hell would I want this piece of shit?"

His bottom lip quivered. Sweat beaded on his forehead like drops of dew. An understated reaction, though his fear smelled like the stink of sweat. "What do you want?"

"Just you, bro." Chuckles bubbled up my throat like acid reflux. "Just you."

It happened fast. Too fast.

Manoj whirled around in his seat, snatched the barrel of the gun, and slammed my arm hard against the center console.

"Hell nah!" I jerked back, adrenaline hitting like a shot of lightning. I punched his face. Blood spurted. His grip loosened. I wrenched the gun free. He recoiled.

I swung again—aiming to cave in his skull—but the butt glanced off.

"Help!" Manoj threw open the car door.

He was halfway out when I snagged the seat belt and wrapped it over his neck. He struggled, but damn he was strong. I kept swinging, kept hitting—until he finally ran out of fight.

As he groaned and bled in the front seat, I stepped out of the car and walked to the driver's side. Nothing but moonlight, gravel, and smokestacks as far as the eye could see. Nothing living. Not even a breeze.

He feebly tried to kick me. Stuffing my gun into my pocket, I grabbed Manoj by one foot and yanked him out onto the gravel. He hit with a thud, knocking the air from his lungs. When he tried to get up, I kicked him in the gut with all my strength and stomped on him, over and over and over.

He curled into a ball, protecting his head and neck.

Panting and flushed, I took a step back and cracked out a laugh before kicking him again. Knots in my stomach that had been there for months were finally untangling.

It had been too long since I'd enjoyed doing my own dirty work. Opal, Cybil, and Lessner had felt like chores, but Manoj was a joy. I'd forgotten how much fun it could be.

Laughing, I took a few steps back for a running start and kicked him right in the face. The noise he made was incredible. Taking a moment to catch my breath, I imagined all the bruises on his internal organs and the pain he must be experiencing.

I didn't want to cause him any permanent damage, but I also hadn't come here just to screw around. I hadn't planned on beating him, but hopefully, he would learn his lesson and do as he was told from here out.

Going into the back seat of the little car, I fetched out the bag I'd placed in there earlier. I used twine for Manoj's hands and ankles—just in case he decided to act up again. His face dripped with blood, hair glistening black in the dim glow of the distant streetlights.

Dragging him into the back seat left me out of breath. I slammed the door, got in the front, and flicked on the child locks. Setting my hands on the wheel, I paused to catch some air. When I looked down, blood was running down my pant leg. In the fight, my gashed thigh had opened back up.

I shook my head but got back to business, adjusting the seat way back for my long legs. Manoj was a little guy, after all. Maybe five-seven with shoes on but skinny as all hell like me.

When I glanced at Manoj again, I realized he was still awake. Faded, broken, and terrified, but still moaning and writhing in pain.

I didn't like the noises he was making anymore, so I snatched a bottle of small, round, white pills from my bag and shoved a handful down his throat.

Perfect.

I clicked on my seat belt, turned the car around, and headed back toward my cabin.

6

Manoj's head bobbed as he faded in and out of consciousness. Fiery pain in his lungs and chest prevented him from passing out—had to be the cracks in his ribs from the man's merciless beating. Every breath was like sucking splinters through a straw down into his lungs.

Thick tears leaked from his crusty eyes and trickled down his bloodstained cheeks. He tried to breathe slowly and evenly through his nose, but that was even worse. The man had reeled back to kick him in the face, and Manoj hadn't turned in time.

Perhaps fighting back had been a bad idea, but he'd been trying to avoid what was happening to him right now. As he'd learned watching crime documentaries with his mother, it was better to die on the street than to be taken to a second location where fates worse than death became the norm.

And where was he now?

Manoj worked for what had seemed like hours to pry open his eyelids, only to be met with flashes of darkness and white light that gave nothing away. But like watching a boat rock on waves, colors began to pool at the corners of his vision, followed by shapes, and finally, the fully formed image of what had to be a basement clarified. It was green outside. Or at least, it looked green through that little broken rectangular window. Trees. And he definitely heard birds twittering.

The sun had cracked the horizon for sure, but it felt very early.

Twine pulling tight on his wrists and ankles was an unfortunate, inescapable reality. He was strapped to a wooden chair, each of his hands tied to an armrest and his legs secured underneath. He pulled at them and tried to rock the chair back and forth before noticing the rusty-brown stain on the concrete not too far away from him.

A smell of raw meat, bowels, and bleach touched his nostrils. With his nose awake, his heartbeat picked up as he studied the stain. His gaze followed the smear back toward the far wall, still partially concealed in shadow where a human-shaped lump lay covered in a sheet of black plastic. Red and brown blood and fluids had oozed out beyond the lumpy canopy, forming a gelatinous puddle.

The air froze in Manoj's lungs. His lips quivered. Over and over again, he asked himself what else could be under the plastic...

But he knew.

Closing his eyes, Manoj fought for a deep breath. All he could seem to manage were snot-coated gasps. From the moment the man said he didn't want the car or money, he'd known something truly horrible was up.

Scenes from every gorenography he'd ever seen flashed through his skull. He tried not to see them, but there was nowhere to hide. Even closing his aching, crusty eyes stung.

Pretending this wasn't happening wasn't going to change anything. He had to keep his cool and think logically.

He was still alive. He supposed he ought to be happy about that. Maybe he could've convinced himself to feel hopeful if he were rich and white, the kind of person the police actually used their resources to find. But he was the son of immigrants—a wage slave with no money, no prospects, no friends in high places. No ransom could be paid, and no cavalry was coming.

The lump of rot and bleach in the corner drew his attention again like a magnet. There was a dead person under there, decomposing. Manoj wondered how many people had been tied to this chair before him. And what was up with the bleach? There was still blood and junk everywhere, plus the dead body.

He had to get out of there.

"Help!" He thrashed from side to side. "Anybody! Please, help! He's going to kill me!"

"You need to be so fucking for real right now." The voice trembled over his skin like the trill of a high-pitched dog whistle. "Shut your face, or I will delete you. I'm not invested. I can quit you whenever I want."

The man was behind him somewhere but close. The sound of approaching footfalls on creaky wood. Stairs, maybe? And then a soft thud over the concrete. Closer and closer.

His voice was wet-sounding and sort of squeaky. Putting that together with flashes he'd gotten of his face and body, Manoj realized he knew him. In the last few weeks, the guy had become a regular at the market. He came in nearly every day and always sat down in the café to eat his lunch and ogle the girls.

"Erik?" Manoj swallowed the lump in his throat.

"You remembered." He sounded pleased by that. "I'm flattered."

"I don't understand. Why are you doing this? I never did

anything to you."

Erik stepped into view, the first rays of dawn spilling over his face.

He was a white dude, tall and skinny, and his hair was currently blond, not brown. He wore black sweatpants and a hoodie with a picture of a green-haired anime chick with big boobs on the front. His face was triangular with a bird-beak nose. Manoj couldn't see the color of his eyes. Just a bit of cloudy white and a reflection of yellow. He was really trying to, though. He wanted to memorize everything about the guy for the police.

"Please. You have to let me go." Manoj fought to keep eye contact, though looking up made him dizzy. "I won't tell anyone about this. I swear. Just—"

"Brother, what?" Erik crossed his arms over his slim chest and shifted his weight to one foot. "Why the hell would I kidnap you just to let you go? That's just stupid."

Manoj blinked a few times, the logical part of his brain buffering. "What do you want from me? What is this place?"

Erik sighed and rolled his eyes, showing a flash of brown in the light. "Don't stress. This is my place. Well, our place, I guess. This is your new crash pad. The basement. Get used to it."

Panic rose in Manoj's throat like vomit, strength surging into his limbs. "What the hell are you talking about?"

"You're mine now. I own you. You're gonna do exactly what I say or...well." He smiled and glanced over his shoulder at the lumpy plastic against the far wall. "I mean, you don't wanna know what went down with the last guy who refused to follow the script. Let's just say his chest looks like a pegboard. Dude was shitting himself before the lights went out. Embarrassing."

Manoj followed his gaze, and his aching stomach did a

painful backflip. Not just from the fate of the victim. He'd never smelled a dead body before. And now that he knew one was there, it was unbearable. "Please. You don't have to do this. People are going to be looking for me."

"Oh, yeah? Like who? Your mom? I'm so scared, bro. Terrified." Erik laughed out loud—raspy and wet all at once.

Manoj's stomach flipped again. "You stay the hell away from my family."

"Or what, bitch?" Erik stepped closer. "Nah, listen. We can do this the hard way, or we can do it the easy way. In the easy way, nobody gets hurt 'cept maybe you. At least not anybody you know personally."

"Why are you doing this? What the hell did I ever do to you?"

"Brother, what? You didn't do shit. You never do shit. You're lame, honestly. You never got anything going on. You're the ultimate boring little beta, for real. That's you, Minage."

Erik pronounced his name wrong, like a lot of people did, to rhyme with *mirage*. Manoj didn't know why, but it pissed him off to an incredible degree.

The bastard continued. "And you're a straight-up klepto. Fillin' your backpack up with cupcakes and batteries and shit."

"How do you know?"

"I got eyes, bro. You really think you're that sneaky? Please." Erik laughed hyena loud, wiping his lips on the back of his hand. As all humor faded from his expression, he leaned down close to look into Manoj's eyes. "I'm finna level with you, okay?"

Manoj didn't answer. But his fingers clenched into fists and the wooden chair creaked.

"You got potential. Like, seriously. You're a slick thief, and

I could use one of those, ya feel me? I know how to steal shit online. I'm freakin' Robin Hood online! Anonymous has got nothin' on me, bro." He smiled proudly, so it even reached his eyes and gave him a dimple. "But I'm too tall and good-looking in person. Too white. So that's where your tiny brown ass comes in. Nobody ever notices you."

Bile pooled in the back of Manoj's throat. He hocked it forward and spat a wobbly yellow lump onto Erik's shoe.

He was aiming for his face.

Erik sneered at the spit, teeth clenching like a predator. "Did you just hock a loogie on my Jordans?"

Anger whipped through Manoj's body. "I won't do anything you tell me!" He yanked at his restraints, thrashing wildly back and forth as they dug into his skin. "Let me go! I'll kill you!"

"Sure, yeah. I'm super motivated now." Erik smacked him across the face so hard his eyes bulged.

Air in his lungs mixed with acid in his guts. Anticipating another slap, Manoj rolled into it and sank his teeth into the offending hand until he tasted blood.

Erik screamed in pain and punched with his other hand. Manoj's jaw slackened. Erik pulled back, stumbling.

"Help!" Manoj cried again. "Help me! Somebody! Help!"

"Shut up!"

Manoj spat out the blood in his cheeks—both Erik's and his own—and shouted even louder. "Help! Help me!"

Standing a few feet back with nothing but fury in his icy eyes, Erik drew a gun from the pocket of his hoodie and pointed it right between Manoj's legs. "I said shut up, or I will put a bullet right in your dick."

Manoj glanced at the high window once again—the trees and the sunlight. It was so close, but it might as well have been a dream. Watching the rustle of green leaves, he wondered again where they were. Out in the middle of nowhere, most likely, where no one could hear him scream.

Once again, his gaze was drawn to the lumpy, leaky pile in the corner. Then, at last, he looked back at the gun pointed directly between his legs.

"That's right." A cruel smile grew on Erik's pointy face. "You're my bitch now, you understand? If you ever, *ever* bite me again, you're done! Dammit, that hurt."

Erik studied the gun in his hand, almost like he'd never seen it before. Without warning, he swung, the hard metal smashing into Manoj's already broken face.

Manoj bit back his outcry of pain and tightened his teeth around the blood pooling in his mouth. "I'll never help you. You may as well kill me now. I will never help you."

"Oh, bet?" Erik cocked his head to one side and grinned like a wild animal. The brown of his eyes held no softness, no hint of humanity. Empty as an open sky. "We'll have to wait and see."

He turned his back and walked out of Manoj's field of vision, which was stained pink now from an open wound on his forehead where the butt had struck. He was dizzy again, even worse than before. He spat out another mouthful of blood.

A moment later, Erik returned with a brand-new roll of duct tape. He dug his nasty, unkempt nail under the cellophane packaging and ripped it off, fighting to get the tape started.

Manoj pulled at his restraints again, but the strength was fleeing him with every labored breath.

Erik pulled out the tape with a loud squeak and creak and stalked closer.

Manoj tried to fight back and make things as hard for him as possible. He took another shot at biting him. But Erik got the tape latched onto his cheek and then used half the damn roll to wrap around and around the back of his head, sealing his lips shut.

"You need to understand that you're my dog. Be good and maybe you'll get a treat. But if you're bad..."

Manoj tried to argue. Erik did another wrap around with the tape, this one even tighter.

"If you're bad, I'll neuter you."

Manoj fought to breathe through his stuffed nose. Blood and snot leaked down over the tape. It wouldn't keep him quiet for long.

"You don't even wanna know what happens to dogs who won't stop biting. Dogs who are just too stupid to learn." Erik smiled with one corner of his lips and stared hard at the lump under the plastic.

The rotting, blood-soaked corpse of a human being this monster murdered.

"There's enough space under there for two." Slowly, Erik's head swiveled back until his lifeless eyes were locked into Manoj's. "Be so for real. I almost want you to try me. See that bitch over there? He tried the hell out of me. Look at him now. Well, look at him!"

Manoj neither blinked nor broke eye contact. If his tongue were still free, he would've unleashed a barrage of profanity. But all he could do was stare.

"Good boy." Erik grinned, as if he'd won something. He dropped the roll of duct tape and walked away—behind Manoj and out of sight. The creak of feet ascending the wooden staircase was followed by the slam of a door.

Manoj thrashed against his restraints. The fear was gone, the dread. All that remained was unfiltered rage. He was not a dog. He wasn't going to beg like one.

He licked at the duct tape and gnawed the fibers—knowing he could eventually get his mouth free. He was amazed he hadn't had an asthma attack yet, but when one inevitably came, he needed to be able to breathe through it.

His inhaler was in his pocket, and he wasn't sure how to get to that quite yet, but one thing at a time. Once his mouth was free, he could chew through the twine to release his hands and feet. Then he could escape.

Erik had signed his own death certificate. He just didn't know it yet.

7

Winter sat across from her husband at the breakfast table, eating Gramma Beth's sugar-soaked cinnamon rolls. Noah hadn't touched his food, which was out of character, as he was usually ravenous in the morning. He'd barely even touched his coffee, so thoroughly engrossed in his laptop was he.

Noah pretty much hadn't slept the night before and was still glowering and snapping at everything. Winter understood without having to ask that his reaction wasn't about the hassle of dealing with their credit cards. He'd been through a traumatic ordeal and, so far, had said nothing to acknowledge it, other than to make jokes. This was about finally expressing some real emotion over his kidnapping. His mutilated hand.

Typical Marine. Laugh when somebody cuts off his finger, pretend like everything's fine and life goes on, then totally lose it over something much smaller.

She stirred her coffee so the edge of the spoon scraped the rim, first clockwise then counterclockwise. "I'm thinking

I'm gonna drive up to Dallas and talk to Erik's former roommate this morning. Joshua Sutherland."

The tapping stopped short, and his green eyes—laced in red from lack of sleep—focused sharply on hers. "Today?"

"They were roommates for almost four years. If I know anything about Erik, he probably gathered a bunch of dirt on Joshua and manipulated him into giving that alibi. Either way, he'll have insights to share. I wanted to go last night, but it'll be easier to track him at his place of work."

"Meaning you feel confident Erik killed his own father."

Winter knew jumping to those kinds of conclusions wasn't detective protocol. She braced herself to get shot down.

Instead, he snapped his laptop closed. "I'll go with you."

Noah agreed with her. Though, now he wanted to join her, her kneejerk reaction was to argue. "Are you sure you'll be able to focus?"

He gave her spider eyes—widening quickly before crushing back into slits. "Am I in trouble?"

"Don't be silly. I just…"

I don't want to be in the car with you for three hours if you're going to be growling and complaining the whole time.

Winter reached across the table, squeezing her husband's hand. What was wrong with her? She was spiraling in so many different directions.

Noah's face softened a little, and he laced his fingers with hers.

"You went through so much. I want you to do what you need to do to get through this. If you need more time to recoup—"

"Stop it." He pulled back his hand. "I'm not letting you out of my sight. I know I said that before, but I mean it this time."

"Right back at you. But if you're coming along—"

"You can drive." His smirk was like ice.

She clenched her teeth to keep in an exasperated sigh. "So you can be on your phone and grumble the whole time?"

"I'm a grown-up, and I can do whatever the hell I want with my phone."

"You know what?" Winter slapped the table as she stood. "I think you should just stay here. I'll bring Ariel. That way, I'm not alone so you won't have to worry."

Before he could respond, she sped out of the kitchen and onto the front porch. The door slammed shut behind her. Winter marched to the railing and strangled it with both hands until the old wood creaked. Her heart hammered, her breath shallow, hands shaking.

When Noah stepped out onto the porch behind her, Winter flinched but didn't look back. Her cheeks burned with a combination of anger and regret, and her eyes swelled with tears. She knew she should be indulgent and understanding, as the last thing he needed was more stress.

But what about her stress? When would she ever get the chance to fall apart without having to immediately yank herself back together?

She knew him too well. The meaning and the hidden pain behind every grunt and sigh stabbed into her like a knife. Every muscle ached.

Noah stepped up behind her and wrapped her up in his arms.

Winter squeaked, the tears in her eyes finally descending as her husband's embrace melted the built-up tension in her body.

Noah cuddled his chin against her shoulder. "I'm sorry."

She spun in his arms and hugged him close, pressing her cheek into the soft cotton of his black t-shirt. He kissed her forehead, which made her squeak again, and her guts got all hot and frothy like a quality cappuccino on a cool spring day.

Butterflies, other people called it, but the way her husband made her feel was so much more than that.

"Can I please come to Dallas?" He pressed his lips into her hair.

Winter laughed and wiped the tears from her cheeks, nodding against his chest. "Yes. But I still want to bring Ariel."

"Are you sure she's ready to come back to work?"

"She said she was. She had an out if she wanted to take it, but she decided she still wanted to be a part of this insanity. I'm not going to handle her with kid gloves anymore. If she's in, she's in. It's time for a crash course."

Noah ran his fingertips through the black wave framing her face. "Does Ariel know that?"

Winter poked him in the belly. "She will when I call her and tell her in a couple of minutes."

8

Winter clutched the wheel with one hand as they sped up I-35 toward Dallas, her phone clenched between her ear and shoulder. Ariel was in the passenger seat, glued to her phone and reading over the case notes Winter had sent before picking her up.

In the back, Noah sprawled in his seat, his uninjured hand tapping out a gentle rhythm to some tune playing in his head.

"I'm sorry," Eve's voice crackled through the fuzzy reception into Winter's ear, "but I can't send you copies of anything from the case file. Since Lessner messed with the federal database, this place is crawling with bureaucrats. I need to sign in triplicate and offer my firstborn as collateral before using federal toilet paper in the ladies' room."

"That sounds...like the reason I'm private these days."

"Don't brag." Eve cleared her throat. The background sound kept shifting as if she were walking, followed by a door closing. When she spoke again, her voice was hushed. "Falkner threatened to pull me from Erik's case."

"What? Why?"

"He's covering his ass. If he finds out I'm sharing federal resources with you and Noah, he's going to take a bigger hit from the ADD. If he takes me off the case, I don't have anything left to share. He's protecting me without saying it."

Winter switched ears, glad she hadn't taken the call on the car's speakers. "Does he know you've already shared information with us?"

"Not yet, but he suspects. Warning me was his way of letting me know to cool it."

"We won't push against that." Winter hoped Eve could hear the gratitude in her voice. "You've done enough to help already. More than we could've asked."

"Bullshit. But thanks for looking out for me anyway."

A brief silence stretched across the airwaves, interrupted by the sound of shuffling papers from Eve's end. "If I was going to tell you anything else, I might mention a freely available website with public information on unsolved cases in La Crosse County, Wisconsin." Noah's phone chimed with a text. "I might've even texted a link."

Winter noticed Noah checking his phone in the rearview mirror. His mouth widened with the first real smile she'd seen on him since yesterday. "Got any more surprises hiding?"

"I might also tell you that the detective who was originally the lead in Benjamin Waller's homicide has since retired from the force as the result of a series of strokes that left him with aphasia and severe memory problems."

"That's...not good."

"To say the very least." Eve scoffed. "I really shouldn't say anything more."

"Got it."

"Except I think we should hang out soon. Like, in person."

"You mean like places where there's no paper trail?"

"I didn't catch that. Static on the line. I think this call might drop."

Eve ended the call, and Winter glanced back at Noah in the rearview again. He sat with his limbs spread, taking up his whole seat, his eyes closed.

Ariel remained fixated on her phone. She looked so different since cutting off her beautiful chocolate curls and dyeing what was left a vivid orange-red hue. Every time Winter turned, it was like seeing her for the first time.

"Ariel, can you look up the cold case file called—"

"Already on it."

Winter shot her an incredulous grimace. "How did you—"

"Noah forwarded the link to me just now, and your phone is super loud."

Glancing at her husband in the mirror again, Winter caught his lips curling into a bigger smile, though his eyes remained closed. "My phone is loud, huh?"

"You got hearing damage, darlin'." Noah offered the comment without opening his eyes.

She furrowed her brow at him in the mirror anyway. "Oh, I do?"

"It's from all the guns that have gone off around you when you didn't wear ear protection." Noah shrugged, still not opening his eyes. "Same for me." He aimed a finger at his left ear. "It's always a little ringy up in here."

"Oh, I didn't realize that." Ariel scrunched up her face. "I just thought hearing got worse when you get old."

Winter's jaw dropped. "Old?"

Blood drained from the young woman's freckled face. "I didn't mean *old*. I mean old-*er*. Like older than me, that's all. I didn't mean—"

"Ariel?"

"Yes, Winter?"

"Shut up."

"You got it." Ariel swung her attention back to her phone. "The report says no fingerprints were found in Benjamin Waller's bedroom except for the victim's and the housekeeper who found him. Erik Waller's prints were found throughout the rest of the house but never in the bedroom."

"Okay." Winter focused on the road, glad to note her vision was still good. It was a nasty blow to find out she was both hard of hearing and old in twenty seconds. On the other hand, she was kind of proud to have lived long enough to be considered "old" by anyone. She'd never once counted on it. "Do we think Erik wasn't allowed in his father's room? Or did he never want to go in there?"

"We don't know."

"How did the killer get in?"

"Through the back door. The glass was broken from the outside, and the killer reached through to unlock it."

"Okay." Winter drummed her fingers on the steering wheel, pinkie to thumb. "How far away was Erik's off-campus residence from the house?"

Ariel's fingers fluttered over the screen as pavement zoomed by. "In current traffic conditions and following the speed limit, it would take four hours and fourteen minutes. Eight hours and twenty-eight minutes both ways, plus however long it would take to commit the crime."

Winter kept on drumming, her vision fading between focusing on the road and her own chewed-down fingernails. She'd been quite cruel to them while Noah was gone.

"Without Joshua Sutherland's testimony, it would be easy to put Erik at the scene." Ariel wriggled in her seat, as if adjusting for comfort. In most U.S. states, a three-hour drive could get you over the state line. Not so much in Texas.

"Absolutely." Winter nodded a few times, bobbing in rhythm to the bump of the wheels.

"Like you said, though, Erik doesn't like to do his own

dirty work." Noah finally opened his eyes and leaned over his knees. "No unidentified prints were found at the scene, which probably means Erik didn't physically do it."

"You think he used somebody else to commit the murder?" Ariel turned in her seat to face him.

"Of course. He likes to sit back and pretend he's a damn chess grand master. We might be on our way to talk to the actual killer right now."

Winter put her thumbnail in her mouth and nibbled. "Did the police take Sutherland's fingerprints?"

"Umm…I don't think so. There's no mention of it in the report."

"I think there's a fair to good chance that Erik's own father was his first victim." Winter bit down on the edge of a hangnail. "That first act is often different from the rest, especially when there's a personal connection. It can offer insight into how someone crosses the line…and what pushes them there."

"Not to mention killers will refine their methods with time and experience." Noah leaned forward to rest a hand on Winter's shoulder.

She reached up and clasped her fingers over his, giving him a slight squeeze. "Maybe Erik manipulated his old roommate into being there with him or simply into lying to give him an alibi. But I can't shake the feeling Erik was also there that night. Even if he wasn't the one holding the knife. I think he was there."

"How can you be so sure?" Ariel turned her big eyes back on Winter. "The evidence doesn't implicate him. If an investigator walks into a situation having already made up their mind, don't they just find evidence to support their own theories? Like tunnel vision."

The skin under Winter's eye twitched. Was Ariel seriously trying to teach her about investigative philosophy?

"Normally, I would agree with you." She kept her voice flat. "But there's a difference between tunnel vision and making reasonable assumptions based on past experiences and known statistics. If a person is murdered on any given Sunday, you look at family, romantic partners, and friends first. And what if you happen to know the victim's son just happens to be a serial killer?"

Sitting back in his seat, Noah let out a breath. "One plus one equals two most of the time."

Ariel's round, childlike eyes caught the sunlight like tiny mirrors. "But isn't it still better to follow the evidence and not make assumptions?"

"If we were simply trying to solve Benjamin Waller's murder, then yes. But that isn't the goal at all."

"It's not?"

"Nope. That's up to the Onalaska PD. Let them worry about staying objective. All I care about is finding Erik. Even if Benjamin Waller's death was just a tragic and unrelated event, I know that following that thread might get us closer to catching Erik…who we know for a fact has killed and mutilated other people."

"Oh." Ariel chewed on her lip. "That makes sense."

"When you get elderly like me, you'll be wise too." Out of the corner of her eye, Winter saw Ariel squirm. "Once Erik's in custody, let the cops and the prosecutors throw the book at him to see what sticks. Even if he only gets convicted for half of what I know he's done, he'll spend the rest of his life in prison."

She cut off her next sentence before it ever started, but even sitting silent in her mouth, the taste was unlike anything she'd ever known before. Like black licorice, it was both spicy-sweet and unpalatably bitter all at once.

Let the prosecutors worry about Erik Waller. Let the prisons. Unless I get to him first.

Winter shook her head, hoping to fling her thoughts from her brain like water from a dog's coat. Yet the feeling and the desire remained.

The prospect of Erik Waller spending his life in prison gave her no satisfaction. She didn't want him humanely punished, but neither did she want him to suffer. She simply didn't want to live in a world where he existed.

When she imagined him standing before her, the only real instinct she felt was to raise her gun and pull the trigger.

Again, Winter shivered back from her own thoughts. She'd never do such a thing. Never, never.

All her life, and especially in her career in law enforcement, she'd always prided herself as someone who upheld the sanctity of even the most despicable human life. She always asked questions first and shot later. It was part of who she was, who she'd promised herself she would always be.

Even when Justin forced her to listen to his endless rhetoric about how much happier she'd be if she simply embraced his way of thinking, she hadn't wavered. He'd spoken of joy. Of utility. Of the satisfaction of taking another person's life. Even then, she'd never once seriously entertained the idea.

Well, maybe once.

Justin was more horrible than any person she knew before or since. But even after everything he put her through, when she had the chance to kill him, she'd held back.

Their final confrontation existed in her memory like an old photo negative.

In that moment, Winter finally saw the truth. The frightening, twisted creature standing in front of her was not her little brother. She couldn't understand how she'd ever tricked herself into thinking he was. He had the same body, the same blue eyes, the same voice, but everything inside him that had ever been worthy of giving or receiving love was already dead.

Erik was different. While Justin had systematically beaten her down until apathy was the only viable emotion, her hatred for Erik burned with the heat of a thousand suns. She didn't want to see him in court or behind bars. She didn't want to give him or anyone else a chance to carry on Justin's revolting legacy. Deep in her heart of hearts, Winter knew that she genuinely wanted to see him dead.

And that thought terrified her.

9

The rest of the drive passed mostly in silence except for the occasional snore from a napping Noah in the back seat or Ariel's fingertips tapping her tablet screen. Winter's thoughts swam from her brother and memories of their final standoff to what she hoped to learn from Erik Waller's college roommate.

Her stomach grumbled as she navigated the nightmarish tangle of pavement that was the greater DFW freeway system. Ignoring the noises from above her beltline, she drove on, finally reaching their destination at just after one o'clock.

Winter found a spot in the shade of a mimosa tree and cut the engine.

The Dallas Center for Fine Arts was a four-story institutional gray building with blue-tinted windows that gleamed in the sunlight. A sign out front advertised youth pottery classes happening that day, and a few yellow balloons tied to it bounced in the hot wind.

"This is the place, I guess." Winter stretched her shoulders and turned her neck to one side until it popped before craning toward the back seat and shaking Noah's knee gently.

Eyes snapping open, he straightened in his seat, his hand dropping to his hip—where he kept his gun. It took a few seconds, but as his hazy eyes sharpened, he gradually relaxed.

Like her, Noah had strong reflexes and a powerful sense of vigilance, which came with the PTSD they shared.

Since his abduction, his reactions to perceived danger had grown more severe.

It's like he just returned from a horrific tour overseas. Back to square one.

Lost in thought, Winter startled when Noah set his hand on hers. As their eyes met, he brushed the edge of her cheek with his fingertips and gave a weak smile. Clearly, she was jumpier than usual too. It was something they could do together as a couple—accidentally scare the hell out of each other while pretending they didn't.

Winter squeezed his hand and wrinkled the skin around her eyes at him. Not trusting herself to speak, she gave a heavy exhale, and they all piled out.

Squinting at the building, Ariel popped on a pair of bright-green polarized sunglasses and squished up her nose. "When I called, they said Sutherland would be in his office today."

Winter nodded, kneeling to secure her gun in her ankle holster. It was just bulky enough to make her leg ache on a long drive if she left it on. "Did you tell him who we are?"

Ariel shook her head. "You said he might be in league with Erik, so I didn't want to spook him."

"Good."

"I said I was a college student interested in running a community education class on watercolors."

Winter and Noah nodded their collective approval, and the three of them crossed the pavement into the building. As they passed through double glass doors, a blast of air-conditioning dried the sweat already beading on Winter's forehead.

The building itself was a kind of intellectual rec center—a library on one floor with a small coffee shop just outside and classrooms filling up the others. The halls were wide with high ceilings, so every noise echoed like the inside of a public pool. They passed by a playground where dozens of children were beating each other senseless with foam blocks and reeling with laughter.

Ariel went to the reception desk while Winter and Noah hung back, vaguely watching the children. Winter's eye was drawn to one little boy—maybe five or six years old—with floppy blond hair and a dinosaur t-shirt. He was skinny and short but seemed to be the ringleader of whatever game they were playing. The boy shouted orders at all the other kids, keeping them organized, making sure everyone was included.

Winter glanced at Noah, who watched the children with a very different expression on his face. A gentle smile and easy posture. A fine mist coated his eyes like starlight on the crest of waves.

"Are you okay?" Winter set a hand between his shoulder blades and leaned closer.

Noah nodded and blinked a few times before turning to her with a forced smile. "Kids are fun, that's all."

She eyed him suspiciously. "I guess they can be."

"Being a grown-up really sucks sometimes."

"So can being a kid."

He crossed his arms and leaned against the gray tiled wall. "I wanted to be an entomologist when I was in second grade. I had a worm farm, and I used to capture crickets and feed them to the praying mantises in my yard."

"Gross." She studied his handsome face. "You never told me that."

"Wasn't meant to be." His gaze still fixed on the kids, Noah swept his fingers over the corners of his mouth. "Why is it that most kids like bugs but most adults are grossed out by them?"

"I knew plenty of kids when I was young who would disagree with that statement." Winter glanced at Ariel, who leaned over the desk as the receptionist showed her something on a piece of paper between them.

"I think kids are less judgmental."

That was the truth…usually. But some kids could be brutal. "You mean those little monsters who will call you old right to your face?"

His eyes smiled. "She's not that young."

Winter opened her mouth to respond but cut herself short as Ariel stepped back from the desk and approached them. "You know where we're headed?"

"Yes, ma'am." Ariel pointed down the hall with one long finger. "Follow me."

"'Ma'am' is something you call a woman twice your age. Stop it with the ageism, or I'll put you in a timeout in the Pilot."

Ariel staggered back. "Oh, I-I'm so sor—"

"I'm kidding." Winter gave her a quick squeeze. "Let's go." Gesturing for her to lead the way, she and Noah followed her assistant down the hall. "I'll run the interview. I want you to record it. And take notes. If there's anything he says that has a whiff of a lie to you, I want you to be able to tell me what and why as soon as the conversation's over."

Ariel's back straightened. She almost looked like she might salute. "You got it, Boss."

Winter winked at her. "'Boss' I can work with."

They rode the elevator to the third floor, exiting into a

carpeted hallway. In a room halfway down, a choir of women practiced a haunting a cappella song in Spanish.

They sang the same words over and over to slightly different melodies, the rhythms and harmonies changing. Winter spoke Spanish with far less than fluent proficiency, but she concentrated and decoded the words one by one.

If the ocean were ink and the sky paper, I could never write how much I love you.

She slipped her hand into Noah's and squeezed. The words could have been written for how she felt about him.

At the end of the hall, they approached an office with the words *Joshua Sutherland* frosted on the glass.

"Fancy. Wonder who he knows to get his own office?" Winter stepped out in front and entered with a gentle tap at the doorjamb to announce herself.

The man looked up. He was in his early twenties with dark, wavy hair. Handsome but in an artsy way. When recognition hit, his eyes bulged like fishbowls.

She'd grown accustomed to that expression over the last few years since Justin made himself famous.

Joshua Sutherland had recognized her, which on its own told her something about him. Winter Black was a bona fide celebrity against her will, but only in one very particular niche. Cops often knew who she was, especially anyone who worked homicide. True crime fans too.

And then there was the other group, comprised of people like Erik Waller.

Winter forced a smile, crinkling the corners of her eyes to make it a bit more authentic. "Hello. Joshua Sutherland?"

"Yes?"

"Thank you for taking the time to see us. My name is Winter Black. I'm a private investigator. This is my assistant, Ariel Joyner, and my husband, Special Agent Noah Dalton." She glanced at each of them in turn. Ariel had her tablet out, one hand fluttering over the on-screen keyboard, and Noah had taken up his position near the door, arms folded across his broad chest to look big and vaguely terrifying.

He hadn't revealed any ID because, technically, he was not operating as a special agent. But Sutherland didn't know that.

"Okaaaay." Sutherland drew out the word in a singsong voice. "What can I do for you?"

"I'd like to talk to you about your relationship with Erik Waller."

His eyebrows popped up, and the color from his face drained. "Erik Waller? Why?"

"You were roommates in college, is that correct?"

"Yeah. But I haven't spoken to him since just before graduation. Did he…" Sutherland cleared his throat and glanced out the window.

Winter watched his face closely, searching for hints of what might be going on inside his mind. He looked startled and disgusted—as if she'd just offered him a slug sandwich for lunch.

He hunched in his seat, his gaze wandering from his desk to his hands to the window. "Did Erik do something bad?"

"He's done a lot of bad things." Noah's interjection came as a rumbling threat, like the earth might start heaving beneath them all at any second.

Sutherland sat up straighter in his seat.

"What did he do?" He cleared his throat again, perhaps to mask a tiny tremble of nerves. Or a lie. "Did he hurt somebody?"

"Yes." Winter looked straight in his eyes. "He's hurt a lot of people."

Whatever blood remained in his face at this point seemed to drain and settle in his fingertips as he pushed aside a coffee mug to fidget with a clicky ballpoint pen. He chewed on his bottom lip and glanced out the window again.

Winter sat quietly for a moment, letting the silence fuel his anxiety. "You don't seem especially surprised by that."

"I'm not." His voice was quiet and gravelly. His dark eyes looked watery, and the pupils had shrunk to tiny pinpricks despite the light in his office.

His sympathetic nervous system, the part responsible for the fight-or-flight response, was in high gear.

What do you want to flee from, Mr. Sutherland?

"Do you know of somebody he hurt?"

Sutherland's body instantly tightened. Everything from his lips to his fingers clenched, and he sat straighter in his chair. "No. I don't think so."

"Were you and Erik friends in college?"

He shook his head. "Erik doesn't have friends."

"That's a bold statement." Winter crossed her legs, revealing the barest hint of the gun on her ankle. She waited for him to elaborate.

He didn't.

"Might I ask how you two ended up living together?"

"Campus housing assigns your roommates. I didn't have any say in the matter. When we moved out of the dorms and started renting a house, he paid the whole deposit and first month's rent, so we just kinda stuck with him, I guess."

"Who else is included in that 'we?'"

"Our other roommate, Mikey Swage."

Ariel piped up but kept her attention on her tablet. "Can you spell that?"

"Like *cage* but with an *SW*."

"Got it. And Mikey's short for Michael, yes?"

He nodded.

Lifting a hand to get Sutherland's attention, Winter brought the conversation back around. "If you'd had any say in selecting your roommates in the dorms, would you have chosen to live with Erik?"

Sutherland shook his head. "No. But he was fine, I guess. Mostly kept to himself."

"Could you tell us what you remember about him from those days?"

"What's this all about? What did he do?"

Noah straightened, filling the doorway with his bulk. "He's wanted for homicide, among other offenses."

Sutherland grimaced. "Like I said, we haven't spoken in months. And even in college, it's not like we hung out or anything. I wasn't home a lot, and he mostly stayed in his room playing video games or studying."

Winter prompted him when he didn't continue. "You said he spent most of his time in his room. Gaming and studying, right?"

"Yeah. He was really smart, on the Dean's List every quarter."

She only begrudgingly admitted to it, but Erik Waller *was* smart, which remained one of the most irritating things about him.

"Do you remember when his father was killed?"

Sutherland clicked his pen a few more times in very slow succession, finally setting it down perfectly parallel with the edge of the desk. "I remember. I mean, it's not every day a guy gets questioned by the police, you know?" He chuckled nervously and glanced at her for less than half a second before looking out the window again. "Erik Waller. Holy shit."

"Where were you and Mikey Swage the night Erik's father was killed?"

"It was the last day of midterms, just before Thanksgiving break. Mikey had finished his classes a little early, and he and some friends flew out to Cabo. He invited me to go, but I already had plans to spend the break with my girlfriend at the time, who was going to school in Wisconsin. That's where I'm from."

"So you and Mikey were friends, but not Erik?"

"Mikey tried to be Erik's friend. He's a good guy. He's so good-looking and popular, you assume he's going to be a total douche, but he actually doesn't have a mean bone in his body. I had to stop hanging out with him after a while, though. Too much partying for me."

Winter glanced at Ariel's furious notes and saw she also had her voice recorder going. "So Mikey was out of the country, and you were in Wisconsin?"

"That's right."

"Where was Erik?"

"Erik stayed at the house. He basically never went away when we had time off. Like I said, he didn't really have any friends. I know he'd never had a girlfriend. He told me once he was saving himself."

"Like for marriage?"

"I guess so." Sutherland shrugged. He seemed to be growing more comfortable the longer they spoke, and doubt itched at Winter. Maybe he wasn't in league with Erik Waller. Either that, or he was a better liar than most people she interviewed.

After he nearly shit himself at the beginning.

Sutherland picked his pen back up. "Mikey invited him to Cabo, but he didn't want to go. He was always kind of a low-key dick about social things."

Noah grunted like a bored bear. "Nothin' low-key about him."

Winter glanced at him where he stood like a sentinel in the doorway, blocking both entry and escape. She turned back to Sutherland. "Do you know how Erik spent his time alone? Did he ever give you an indication he had other friends he hung out with?"

"Not a chance. Dude lived in his room, seriously, either studying or gaming. He had a huge curved-screen setup. PC games, of course. And VR before it really became a thing. His room was like walking onto the bridge of a spaceship. His TV took up a whole wall. Made sense, though, given his dad ran Yorobo."

"You saw the inside of his room?"

He nodded. "Yeah, one time he invited me in to play a first-person shooter, some zombie game. I played once and never gamed with him again after that."

Winter nodded. Addiction to video games explained the way Erik spoke, always treating his crimes like contests and quests.

The line between reality and fantasy had become so blurred that Erik either didn't know the difference anymore or he didn't want to know. He didn't see other people as real. They were all NPCs, each with an objective stamped on their foreheads.

"If you were in Wisconsin that night," Winter said, bringing the focus back to the matter at hand, "how is it you were able to provide an alibi for Erik when he was in his room back in Chicago?"

Sutherland leaned in. "So I take a Greyhound all the way up to Green Bay, right? But I'd only been at my girlfriend's place for like an hour when I get a text message from a random number saying that she was cheating on me. For three months. I guess his bro code kicked in. And the guy sent me pictures of the two of them together."

Winter perked up. "Did you ever meet him in person?"

He looked very uncomfortable—like someone was jabbing the bottoms of his feet with Legos. "The dude she was cheating on me with? Nah. It's not like we became buds or something."

"Did you ever text the person with the random number again after that?"

"No. I didn't want to know anything more. I wasn't gonna play that bullshit game again. She ripped my damn heart out, so I just wanted to get away from her, and I hopped on the next bus back to Chicago."

Winter nodded along, wondering how Erik might've been involved. Surveillance was the name of the game with him. If Erik found Sutherland's girlfriend was cheating on him, he never would've come straight out with the information. He would've kept it out of sight, deep in his pockets with all the other secrets he'd collected, only exposing them to better serve his own interests when the time was right.

"Did you ever actually speak to the other man, or was the communication only through text?"

"Text."

"Do you remember his name?"

Sutherland gritted his teeth. "Sure do. I wish I didn't. But it's kind of hard to forget a name like Ernst Zippler."

"And what was your ex's name?"

"Gloria Allen. Though I don't see why that should matter."

"There's no such thing as too much information when dealing with a homicide." Winter showed him her empathy lips—a kind of upside-down smile that silently conveyed how much she wasn't enjoying this. "What time did you leave Green Bay then?"

"I was only in Wisconsin for a few hours. It's, like, a four-hour ride back. I caught the last bus at around ten and got back home at, like, two in the morning."

Winter drummed her fingers lightly on her leg and nodded. "Go on."

Sutherland ran his hand through his hair. "I walked from the bus station. When I got home, Erik was asleep on the couch in the living room with the TV on. I just turned it off and went to my room."

"He wasn't sleeping in his room? I thought he spent most of his time in his room. Wasn't that odd?"

"Oh, yeah, right before midterms, his whole entertainment system went on the fritz, so me and Mikey had to deal with him camping on the couch every night and zoning out to reality TV."

"Did you ever speak to Gloria Allen or Ernst Zippler again?"

"Nope. Blocked her." Sutherland sounded proud. "The police showed up the next morning to talk to Erik, and they took both of us down to the station for interviews. I had the feeling they thought Erik was involved somehow. I told them exactly what I just told you, and I guess in the end, that was enough to let him off the hook."

"Do you think he's innocent?"

Sutherland's gaze snapped to her face. "Considering he was in Chicago the whole time, kinda hard to imagine him being guilty."

"But you were in Wisconsin."

"What the hell is that supposed to mean?"

"Just an observation." Winter kept her expression neutral and her eyes on his. "It's an interesting coincidence that Erik's alibi conveniently came home right when he needed him."

"I was on a bus half the night."

"Did the police ask to see your ticket? Did they speak to Gloria to verify your story?"

"Of course they did! I can't believe this." Sutherland wiped a hand over his face in frustration. "Are you seriously trying to suggest *I* had something to do with what happened to Mr. Waller?"

Winter didn't respond.

"That just doesn't make sense. Neither of us even had a car. How the hell would we even do it? And why? I would never."

"Did Mikey have a car?"

Sutherland's jaw hung slightly open, twitching from side to side. "Yeah."

"I'm assuming he didn't take it with him to Cabo."

"Well, yeah, but we didn't have access to it."

"He took his keys with him?"

Sutherland threw his arms in the air in frustration. "Shit, lady. I don't know."

"You're going to keep your tone respectful when speaking to my wife." Noah angled his chest to Sutherland. It didn't sound like a request or even a threat, just a simple fact of life.

The man swallowed hard enough that it made a noise. "Erik could've taken Mikey's car, I guess. I don't know. Mikey might've even given him permission to drive it. He was kinda dumb like that."

"What kind of car did Mikey drive?"

"A powder blue 1987 Chevette." A nostalgic smile played around his eyes, in spite of the worried grimace Noah had inspired. "I remember 'cause we all used to make fun of what a rusted-out hunk of junk it was." Sutherland fiddled with a braided leather bracelet on his wrist. "Why are you asking me about this now? Did you find new evidence or something?"

"Something." Winter had been hoping he wouldn't ask that question. "Erik's on the run right now. He's armed and extremely dangerous. We also need to tell you that, as far as we know, he's currently in Texas."

The poor man's eyes nearly popped out. For the first

time, Winter could see his fear like sparks of electricity in the atmosphere. "He's here? Why?"

"I think you might have an idea." Winter closed her mouth and leaned back in her chair, allowing silence to fill the room. Sometimes, the best thing an interviewer could do was sit and say nothing. Uncomfortable silence was far more powerful than many people realized, especially when dealing with a nervous individual. They would spill every bean they had in an attempt to escape it.

"I know who you are," Sutherland said at last.

Fixing her expression into a frown, Winter studied his twitching lips, his bloodless cheeks. Once she caught his dark eyes, she held fast and lifted her brows in question.

Sutherland shifted in his seat, his gaze flitting about the office like he was watching an invisible fly. "Erik's obsessed with you."

"Why?"

"Because you're Winter Black." He bit his lip and pressed a sweaty palm flush to his desk. "Justin's sister."

10

When the word *Justin* left Joshua Sutherland's mouth, Noah's heart rate picked up and his jaw clenched. He knew from experience that standing behind Winter and looking vaguely like he might snap and start breaking bones at any second was a rather effective interrogation technique, having worked so many times in the past.

But his job description shifted whenever Justin's name came up. When the muscles tightened in Winter's face, his body suffered physical pangs of need to protect her.

Noah kept his back straight and his gaze fixed on Sutherland, even as he stepped up behind Winter and laid his good hand on the back of her chair.

The guy seemed nervous—frightened even. Noah got the distinct sense that Joshua already knew what Erik Waller might be capable of, even if he seemed surprised at the mention of the word *homicide*.

Or was Sutherland nervous because he was knowingly involved in Erik's plans?

"How do you know who I am?" Winter's dark-pink lips

pressed into a serpentine smile, and she tilted her chin slightly.

"You're famous."

"Only in certain circles."

"You can't watch the ID network longer than a few hours without seeing your face."

Winter's smile turned frosty. "Are you a big fan of true crime, Joshua?"

Everyone in the room suffered a shiver from the withering tone in her voice. Time and again, she proved herself a shape-shifter—one moment warm and loving, the next as ice-cold and unforgiving as a tundra.

Sutherland wiped his sweaty hand over an even sweatier neck. "I used to be."

Winter waited in silence, watching him twitch. Noah knew exactly what she was doing, comfortable in any space that his wife created. But Sutherland clearly had no tolerance for it. Even Ariel began to squirm.

"I got a psychology minor while I studied the arts," Sutherland was back to fidgeting with his pen. "When I took Abnormal Forensic Psychology, we studied the motivations of violence."

Noah shifted his weight from one foot to the other. Watching, waiting.

Sutherland exhaled. "Our assignment was to compare and contrast serial killers, mass murderers, and sadists with so-called ordinary people who were compelled to perform many of the same behaviors as participants in state-sanctioned violence. Like, what is the difference in psychology between someone like Ted Bundy and some random dude in the Marines killing Al Qaeda operatives in Afghanistan?"

Stiffening and coming around Winter's chair, Noah glared down at the shifty-eyed younger man behind the desk.

"Now that you're face-to-face with a Marine who served in Afghanistan, why don't you describe the differences you see?"

Winter cleared her throat behind him, and Noah let out a breath, relaxing but keeping his steely glare on Sutherland, who fidgeted with that same pen until it finally tumbled to the floor. When he collected the pen and sat back up, he avoided looking at Noah, seeming to prefer Winter's icy stare instead.

"What did your psychology coursework have to do with me, Joshua?"

"We had to pick a case study and write an evaluation of the subject's mental state based on available data. I picked… well, you."

Winter's neck tightened. Noah wanted to snatch Sutherland by his collar and beat his head against his desk.

"You picked me?" Winter spat out her words like poison. "Do you think I'm a sadist?"

"No! I didn't mean that." His gaze jumped from Winter to Noah and back again. "History isn't really my bag. Too much propaganda to sort through. I wanted a more recent example. A case study where there were two killers on scene with two different motives. The Stewart case was ideal."

"Two killers," Winter whispered.

He had the grace to look apologetic. "But two very different motives. Your brother was focused on control and coercion. You…were focused on survival."

Noah moved his hand from the chair to his wife's shoulder and squeezed, hoping to lend her some grounding. She never wanted to talk about what happened that day—not with him, not with anyone. Unfortunately, the worst day of her life had been recorded for posterity and was still available to play on repeat on the dark web. The day Winter was forced at gunpoint to murder a husband and a wife right in front of their young child and the corpse of their older daughter.

"I've always been fascinated by the dynamics of authority and compliance," Sutherland continued, clearly failing to read the room. "Justin was the perfect case study. I wanted to understand his army of fans, the people that protested outside the courthouse during his trial. Justin Black is the first real serial killer of the social media age. He made so many people a part of all the horrible things he did. Like he was producing a TV show about murder."

Noah's fist tried to clench in his pocket, intensifying the dull ache in his missing digit. His jaw tightened. "Are you a fan?"

"God, no!" Sutherland responded so quickly that a bit of spittle flew from his lips. "It's just, individual monsters aren't so unusual, but when a whole section of the population supports a monster, things get interesting. True abnormal psychology is rare. But the potential for evil within the average person is universal. I studied the link between those voyeuristic tendencies and whether those who possess them are more easily influenced to commit real-life violence."

"I'd like to read your paper." Winter's voice was flat and monotone, her back stiff.

"Really?" Sutherland's face brightened, but only for a second before he seemed to recognize how inappropriate that was. "I could email it to you."

She fished through her bag to find her business cards and set one on the desk in front of him.

He picked up the card and scrutinized it, his head bobbing. Licking his lips, he flicked his gaze to Winter, quickly moving down her body and back up. It was so fast and so subtle, Noah doubted if she even noticed, but *he* certainly did.

Even while being interrogated, the little nerd couldn't

help checking her out. There was a time when Noah would've gotten angry about that, but such were the hazards of having a smoking-hot wife.

"What does any of this have to do with Erik being obsessed with my wife?"

Sutherland glanced at Noah—not even his face but his chest—before refocusing on his desk. "Erik walked in on me one day while I was on one of Justin's fan sites, reading through chat boards. He knew who Justin was and was excited to have somebody to talk to about it. I wanted to talk about it, too, since I was deep in the trenches at the time. That was the closest we ever came to connecting."

"And…?" Winter prompted.

Sutherland sipped his coffee. "And a lot of people knew who Justin was, so I didn't think it was weird, especially since Erik was a horror nut. But as we talked, I noticed how excited he was about the whole thing. Like, bouncing around the room and getting loud. It wasn't like him at all. He was usually so quiet. I got the impression he'd been following the case really closely. He knew details I hadn't even dug up at that point. At first, it was just weird, and then…"

Winter drummed her fingers on the side of her thigh, waiting. Noah took his cues from her and stared hard at Sutherland.

Rising from his seat, the man paced to the window and turned his back. "One day, Erik told me he'd joined one of the chat rooms. He got confused when I wasn't excited about it. He tried to show me some of Justin's OG content and got really mad when I refused to watch it with him."

"You never actually watched any of the videos?"

Sutherland visibly shivered and turned again to face them. "Hell, no. I can't even watch regular horror movies where I know it's all fake. I don't know why anybody would want to watch something like that. But since I was still researching the psychology of someone who would, I kinda started looking at the whole thing with Erik like another case study."

"You wrote about Erik's obsession with my brother?"

"Not by name or anything. I just used him as a model for the kind of men who subscribed to Justin's channel."

Winter scooched to the edge of her seat, rapt. "This is that same paper?"

"Uh-huh."

"I truly can't wait to read it."

"Well, now I'm nervous." He chuckled as if to prove the point, but there was something vaguely flirtatious about it. "I wrote it as an undergrad. What if it sucks?"

Noah took the empty seat at Winter's side, setting his hands on his lap so the good one covered the injured one. He adjusted his eyes to make sure Sutherland would see the threat of murder written there.

"Do you, by chance, remember Erik's username on the fan page?"

"Yes." He stretched his lips, looking uncomfortable. "It was *Juswinterik*." Sutherland spelled it out.

Noah worked hard to keep from clenching both fists again. Sutherland was simply acting like a man in the presence of a very attractive woman. Noah needed to direct his real anger toward Erik Waller.

With every fiber of his being, he wished he could go back to that day in the park when the psychopath had brazenly introduced himself…and strangle the life out of him.

"I noticed him getting deeper into the whole thing the more we talked." Sutherland hunched his shoulders. "I don't think he knew about the chat rooms before we went on the website together. I think he knew about Justin mostly from TV. And he only knew you by name. But when I…um… I mean, this is awkward. I'm sorry."

Noah lifted his chin and narrowed his eyes. "Spit it out."

"I remember the day Erik told me he'd watched the video of what happened to the Stewarts. He fell in love with you that day."

"Fell in love?" Noah echoed, incredulous.

"In the Greek goddess sense, you know what I mean? He even printed off a picture and kept it in a frame next to his bed."

"He did *what*?" Fury boiled like acid in Noah's blood. He rose from the seat he'd just taken and began to pace behind Winter and Ariel. He felt like a predator locked in a cage, his stomach trembling with hunger, his prey just beyond reach. "That dirty son of a—"

"I used to own a video camera." Sutherland stared at his feet and picked at a tiny hole in his jeans right near the coin pocket.

Winter squished up her nose. "What?"

"I had this camera my mom gave me. I kept it in my closet at the house and never really used it. It was too much work."

"I really hope this has a point," Noah snarled. He was done having this conversation and done being in this tiny room. If he didn't find Erik soon and strangle him with his own intestines, he was pretty sure his body would soon implode from the pressure.

"When I moved out after graduation, I was packing up the closet, and I noticed the box the camera was in was open. I'm super anal about that kind of stuff, so I knew somebody else had used it."

"You think Erik?"

He nodded and resumed his seat at the desk. He crossed an ankle over his knee and bounced his foot fretfully. "I took everything out of the case to put it away properly, and I noticed some dried gunk on the lens and gumming up the swivel hinge on the screen. I cleaned it with some alcohol wipes, and it was…red. It looked like…I mean, I thought it might be—"

"Blood?" Winter offered.

His wide eyes met hers. "I never could be sure. But I also noticed one of my SD cards was missing. I talked to Mikey, and he didn't know anything. And I knew he wouldn't take anything without asking. He wasn't that kind of guy."

"Did you ask Erik?"

"He laughed it off. He said if he wanted a camera, he'd buy one, and mine was a piece of crap anyway."

"You think he was lying?"

"I know he was."

Noah made no attempt to hide his confusion. "Erik had a lot of money, right? He could've just bought his own."

Sutherland shook his head. "Well, yeah. He was always a rich boy, and after his dad died, he inherited everything. Still, I know he used my camera. I know he was the one who got the smudge on it. And I know he stole my SD card. But I was leaving anyway and kinda just glad to be rid of him, so I let it go."

"Did you tell the police?" Winter asked.

He shook his head. "It's not like the camera was missing. And it was just a smudge. Besides, this was a solid month after."

"After what?"

"After Erik's father was killed."

Winter sighed in disappointment. "Do you still have the camera?"

"Donated it to a thrift store a few months ago. I don't really remember when exactly or which store."

Winter's nose twitched a few times. Then she nodded resolutely and rose from her chair. "Thank you for your time. I think that's all the questions we have right now." She aimed a finger at her business card on his desk. "If you think of anything else, please contact me. And I really would like to read your paper."

"You got it. I'll send it over right now." Sutherland offered his hand, and they shook. Ariel did the same. When it was Noah's turn, he made a conscious effort not to crush Sutherland's hand to a pulp.

"Good luck." Joshua gave a little wave. "I hope you catch him."

With a mouthed *thank you*, Winter turned on her heel and left the office, with Ariel at her back.

Noah hovered over Sutherland's desk, staring down at him. "If you were involved in any of this, we'll find out. I'm only going to give you this last chance to come clean."

Sutherland's watery, bulging eyes snapped up at Noah as his bottom lip trembled. "What?"

"Is there anything more you think we ought to know?"

His gaze darted around again. He shook his head.

Noah stayed in place for another moment, glowering down at the twitchy young man. Before he could allow himself say another word, he turned and followed his wife into the hall.

11

On the way back to Austin, after a stop in Waco for dinner, Winter was grateful when Noah insisted on taking the wheel so she could read. The conversation with Joshua Sutherland had left her unsettled, her brain overflowing with new unanswered questions. She sat in the passenger seat with her phone up under her nose, studying the academic paper.

Subject B presents an intriguing variable to the 'destructive obedience' paradigm. Though Subject A is the de facto authority figure in this situation—leading by coercion, threat, and drugging—Subject B's own familial position in relation to Subject A as the elder sibling indicates that a sense of empathy and responsibility for Subject A may have been contributing psychological factors in Subject B's cooperation.

Winter set her phone down. She wanted to throw it. Instead, her knuckles turned white around the phone case.

"You all right?"

"Sutherland's just full of shit." She didn't feel empathy or responsibility for Justin. Well, she did, but she didn't. She blinked away a memory flash of Justin. Her brother wearing

SpongeBob pajamas. No. He was responsible for his own actions—his own horrible actions.

And I am responsible for mine.

She wouldn't dwell on Sutherland's evaluation of events he was not party to. He was only one of many sideline shrinks trying to overexplain the painfully obvious—abuse created abuse. The Preacher created Justin, and Justin...well, Justin created crime and mayhem and brand-new psychopaths all the way down.

Winter closed the paper and switched to her map app. If she was going to stop Justin's newest psychopath, she had to understand what Erik had done.

She reviewed the routes between Erik Waller's rental house in Chicago and Benjamin Waller's home in Onalaska.

Joshua Sutherland had left for Green Bay that afternoon and returned home between two and two thirty the following morning. He was gone for maybe a dozen hours. The M.E. who examined Benjamin Waller's body had put the time of death between eight p.m. and six a.m.

If all those facts were indeed true, and if Erik had gained access to a vehicle—Mikey Swage's Chevy Chevette—he would've had just enough time to commit the crime himself. It was about five and a half hours from Chicago to Onalaska one way, or eleven hours roundtrip. Erik even had time to film his father's murder, especially if he'd had an accomplice.

Ariel leaned forward over the center console. "Do you think he was telling the truth?"

Winter shifted to look at her. "I do, actually."

Keeping his eyes on the road, Noah echoed the sentiment. "So do I."

One problem kept nagging at her. "What I don't understand is why the original investigators would've simply accepted Erik's alibi."

Ariel shrugged. "They would've looked deeper if they'd

found evidence linking Erik to the scene. Whether or not his alibi is rock-solid doesn't really matter if they don't have any other evidence to accuse him."

"I'm afraid you're right." Winter huffed out her exasperation. "Okay, so let's just pretend for a minute that Erik's guilty and that he killed his father with his own hands. How did he do it?"

"*If* he did it, he probably used Mikey Swage's car."

"Not a lot of Chevettes on the road these days." Noah hit the brake as a semi crossed into their lane. "Maybe we could catch it on some old security camera footage."

Ariel scoffed. "The police in Wisconsin would've checked that at the time, surely."

"You'd be surprised the obvious things that fall through the cracks in an investigation." Noah reached up and adjusted the rearview, presumably to see over Ariel's bobbing head. "Especially when we're dealing with a crime that might've crossed state lines. Was the FBI involved in the investigation at all?"

"Not from what I saw in the public case file. The local PD in Wisconsin handled the investigation, with cooperation from Chicago."

Winter didn't like any of this. "I feel like we're getting sidetracked."

"*If* Erik is guilty, then he must've planned on using Sutherland for an alibi." Noah glanced over his shoulder as he changed lanes to pass a very slow-moving Winnebago. "How could he possibly know he'd be back just in time to confirm his alibi or be home at all? How'd he even know with certainty that Sutherland would hop on a bus back to school?"

"The timing of finding out about his cheating girlfriend is pretty suspicious, but it's a gamble to know if Sutherland would come back at the exact moment he'd need an alibi."

Winter tossed out a theory that'd been playing over and over in her mind. "What if the other guy was Erik?"

Ariel narrowed her eyes into slits and stared at Winter from under her thick lashes. "You think Erik was sleeping with Sutherland's girlfriend, Gloria Allen?"

"No. I think Erik found out about a genuine affair the girlfriend had, probably because he was monitoring his roommates. And I think he might've been the one who decided when and how the affair came out. Sutherland said the guy sent him pictures as proof. I'd bet you a thousand dollars Erik's the one who took those pictures, and he sat on them until the time was right."

"You got all that from what that dude just said?" Ariel blinked a few times in quick succession—an outward sign of a buffering brain. "How?"

"I know Erik. I know how he operates. He's a master manipulator. He pays attention, and he knows what buttons he needs to press. If he needed Sutherland home at a certain time, he would've known just which seeds to plant and when to plant them."

Noah set the cruise control and leaned back in his seat. "Erik collected the evidence, planned the murder, and waited for the holiday break to provide him the best opportunity. He texted Sutherland the photos, pretending he was the guy his girlfriend was having an affair with, which he knew would send him on his way back home."

"But how would he know that?" Ariel threw an arm in the air. "How did he know Joshua Sutherland wouldn't stay and argue? Or that he wouldn't forgive her?"

"You can't push people's buttons if you don't know how they're going to react." Winter shrugged and glanced out the window at the passing fields of cattle. "Erik had spent enough time with Sutherland, observing him, to be able to predict his behavior."

"Then Erik drove Mikey Swage's car to Onalaska and killed his dad. At some point before or after, he texted Sutherland, but either way, he had plenty of time to get home and pass out on the couch."

Winter smiled at her husband. It sounded a bit silly saying it all at once, but Erik Waller was nothing if not convoluted. "Unless Sutherland was lying about everything."

"Maybe Swage was the one working with him."

"I doubt it. The cops in Wisconsin must've put him in Cabo. Ariel?"

Her fingers padded away at her tablet, and she made a dull noise in her throat like an old furnace about to kick on. "Yes. His whereabouts were confirmed."

Winter loosened her seat belt so she could turn even more. "Have you found him?"

"I'm searching for him right now."

"How about the girlfriend? Gloria Allen? Or this Ernst Zippler? Sounds like a made-up name if there ever was one."

"Still looking." Ariel harrumphed and swiped a hand over her hair, pushing back her baby bangs.

"I'm leaning toward believing Sutherland, but I also believed Cybil Kerie, so what the hell do I know?" Winter grunted and let her chin fall into her hand, her elbow propped up on one knee.

"Don't do that." Noah put his bandaged hand on the wheel and set his right hand on her knee. "You try to give people the benefit of the doubt. Maybe it gets us into trouble sometimes, but the fact that you can still do that after everything you've been through is part of what makes you my favorite person."

Winter wasn't convinced by anything he'd just said, but she loved him for saying it. The brief glimpses she got of herself through his eyes were better than any therapy.

Ariel laughed under her breath. "Damn, Winter. I can see

why you locked him down. Where can I get me one, hmm? Do I have to join the FBI?"

"No, not necessarily." Winter laced her fingers through his. "Sometimes a good one falls through the cracks. Could happen in any line of work."

Noah kissed her knuckles, smoothing out some of the twisted thorns digging into her guts.

Her phone buzzed, startling her. "It's Darnell." Winter swiped to answer. "Hello?"

"We found a body in the trunk of an abandoned car in the precinct parking lot about an hour ago."

Winter had to laugh at the absurdity of starting a conversation in such a way. "Who is this?"

"Very funny, Black. Harlan Lessner. He's dead." Darnell's deep voice was slow and full of gravel, cutting off any last bit of humor. "He was murdered. And his body was stuffed into the trunk of a car driven by a missing nineteen-year-old."

12

My hands trembled as I fought with the childproof cap on the little orange bottle. Pathetic. I hated when my body betrayed me like this—shaking like a leaf when I needed precision, clarity, control.

When the damn cap finally gave way, I tipped the bottle back, letting the three remaining pink pills slide onto my tongue. Time to re-up soon.

The pain in my leg pulsed with every heartbeat, worsening by the hour. I hadn't looked at it since yesterday—hadn't needed to. The yellow pus, the red lumps spreading around the wound…I didn't need a degree to know it was infected.

I had to get stronger antibiotics. I'd add them to my next dark web drug order. No big deal. I'd be fine. I *had* to be.

But the stairs? They were getting old. Especially after Lessner broke the damn railing crashing me into it. Dick.

And Manoj…

That bastard was turning out to be a real disappointment. I'd expected obedience, maybe some fear-fueled loyalty.

Instead, I got lip. Resistance. Breaking him was taking longer than I wanted, and time was not a luxury I could spare.

Groaning like an old man, I dropped onto a wobbly wooden chair, every movement dragging pain across my thigh like a serrated blade. Shadows sliced the basement in long, jagged lines—striping Manoj's unconscious face and stretching across the dried blood where Lessner had bled out.

Even out of the basement, the guy still stank. His bloated corpse was currently baking in the trunk of a car, but its putrid ghost remained in this room.

"Stupid son of a bitch." I pressed a hand to the gash in my leg. It didn't dull the pain. Just shifted it—turned the constant throb into a sharper, meaner sting.

I welcomed it. Let it focus me.

My chest burned with every breath, and pressure pounded behind my eyes like a war drum. I hadn't wanted to kill him. Not really. Had I?

Doesn't matter. He gave me no choice.

And now, with my inside man gone and his corpse marinating in the trunk, I was the one stuck cleaning up the mess.

My jaw clenched hard enough to crack enamel as I replayed Lessner's final words. That smug prick thought dragging my father into it would get a rise out of me. It did.

Big mistake.

Of all the deaths stacked like notches in the back of my mind, I'd only personally delivered four—Opal Whatever, Cybil Kerie, Harlan Lessner, and, of course…the one that started it all.

She never even had a chance.

My mother died the day I was born—amniotic fluid embolism during an emergency cesarean. A medical fluke.

But my father never saw it that way. He blamed me. Said it out loud when I was eleven.

"I wish she'd lived instead of you. I loved her. You? You're just a cruel joke from a sadistic god."

He locked me in my room for the millionth time after that. I'd sit there, all alone, wishing I hadn't killed my mother. I wanted to go back in time and kill myself instead.

I once had a babysitter who actually cared about me. An old woman called Ruth who carried spicy Mexican lollipops in her purse. She had one of those nasty little squish-face dogs—a ball of white fluff with loud, obstructed airways. Ruth used to sit on the couch with me and play with my hair while we watched old Disney movies. And she always smelled like stale popcorn.

I'll never forget the first time we watched *Snow White and the Seven Dwarves*. I liked the evil queen a lot—her magic and mercilessness. The dungeon she kept under her castle full of the skeletons of her enemies. The cute little box she gave to the huntsman to hold a human heart.

After watching the movie dozens of times, I realized something that most people didn't and never would. Snow White and the evil queen were actually the same person.

One was the young, naive version—a born victim too stupid to know what was good for her. The evil queen was the woman she grew into after she finally let that part of herself die. Eating the poison apple was a transformative act. One pathetic, useless woman died so a wiser, more magical, more powerful one could take her place.

That mirror on the wall was right that the fresh woman was fairer than the old and jaded one, but it was very, very wrong about who was the most beautiful. The truest beauty was in the transition. Death of the one and birth of the other. Only after experiencing that death was Snow actually ready to join her prince and become his evil queen.

I used to fantasize about finding a coffin in the woods with a beautiful woman inside. No heartbeat and cold to the touch. One who'd been waiting for me for years, caught in this transition and surrounded by lesser men who lacked the power to pull her through.

Winter had been languishing in her glass coffin. Justin was the one who killed her inner Snow White. I was lucky enough to witness it, at least on video. Laying her hands on the Stewarts and snapping their necks was her version of biting the poison apple.

For nearly a year, I'd dreamed about her nearly every night. I'd come upon her in the woods, looking so beautiful. So many times in my dreams, I'd kissed her dead lips and waited for her to rise, but she never once opened her eyes for me. It used to drive me insane. I'd wake in the morning ready to hunt her down and cut her eyes out just to get a good look at their color. But the longer I resisted that temptation, the easier it became to be patient.

Now the moment I'd been planning for was so close. Winter would finally see me. I would stand in front of her, kiss her lips, and watch as she completed her transition into the woman she was always meant to be. My evil queen.

That was my magic—the power I'd been born with.

As I got older, I realized I knew something about death that most people didn't. And that was simply how easy and common and uneventful it was. I came to understand myself as an agent of death. Like winter and old age, I existed to move creatures and souls from one state of being to another. To transform them into their final form. That was my purpose. It didn't matter if I fully understood why. The mission was the mission whether or not it made sense.

I wanted to learn how to use my power.

The way that little squished-face dog had tried to get away…Ruth hadn't wanted to be my babysitter after that.

The pills began taking effect, the world gently twirling like an eddy in a stream. My head slumped back to rest on the concrete wall, and I closed my eyes. My dad used to bring me to a cabin in the Midwest in the summers, which meant neither Lessner nor Manoj were the first to be trapped in a basement in the woods in the middle of nowhere.

All my life, I never once felt like I belonged anywhere. Even when I started college and finally got away from my old man, I didn't fit in. My roommates were nicer to me than anyone had ever been, but even they only ever approached me with caution. I was all alone in the world. No one had ever understood me.

And then I found Justin Black, aka The Prodigy, aka one of the most prolific American serial killers of the twenty-first century. Reading about the things he did was exhilarating and inspiring. Being in the chat rooms on his fan sites filled me with a sense of community unlike anything I'd ever known. Watching the videos…I grew so excited, I couldn't even think straight.

Before Justin, I'd never known someone who shared my magic. Someone born for the purpose of bringing death to others. I read his manifestos and listened to his speeches—all available on the site for a small fee. Most importantly, I watched his work. The first time I saw him drive a knife into a woman's chest and twist, I felt seen. I knew I was ready to eat my own poison and begin my transition into the man I was always meant to be.

The more I watched Justin and the more I learned about him, the more I came to understand his obsession with family. Everything he did—from torturing his sister to kidnapping Timothy Stewart—was motivated by a deep, compulsive need to be a part of a normal nuclear family.

He wanted a wife and a son—people he could count on always having his back and who would help him in his mission. Most people misunderstood that about him. They thought he was wild and destructive just for the sake of it. Only I saw that he was trying to build something new.

Looking at Justin, and especially at Winter with her ice-blue eyes, I knew in my heart that I was the missing piece in all of Justin's plans. Had I been there with him, cleaning up after his stupid mistakes and keeping him on course so he didn't get distracted by pointless side quests, he never would've been caught.

Really, it wasn't that hard to avoid capture. I couldn't understand why it kept happening to every idiot I persuaded to work for me.

It took weeks for me to build up the courage to write a post addressed directly to him. I knew he was able to get online sometimes and interact with the community, even though he was locked up. Turned out that all had to do with the green stuff, just like everything else.

One of Justin's guards—and nobody seemed to know who exactly—was happy to let the iconic serial killer get online if the price was right. A price steep enough to keep out all the rabble, but easy for a rich boy who'd already hacked into his father's brokerage account.

Finding the site where I could "donate" was exponentially harder than stealing ten thousand dollars from my father. Once the transaction cleared, I received access codes to a chat forum, along with a date and time when I could expect Justin to connect with me.

I spent days typing up my initial message, trying to make it perfect. I told him about my theory of Snow White and rebirth. What his work meant to me and how it inspired me. Finally, I confessed my feelings about him and his sister, and how if he ever wanted to succeed again, he would need me as a cornerstone in his new family.

Justin's response came back in less than five minutes. Three words.

Prove it, bitch.

For weeks, I agonized over what he meant. Did he want me to prove that I really wanted to be a part of his family? That I didn't care about my own? Or did he need me to prove that I had what it took?

I remembered sitting at the kitchen table thinking about all this when my father walked in and bitched at me for not cleaning up after myself. He called me useless, and the answer hit me all at once. I knew what I had to do.

Over the next handful of weeks, I researched my plan in exacting detail. First, I stole the key to my roommate's Chevette and made a copy while he was asleep. I knew one or both of my roommates would be my most convincing alibi, as I wasn't exactly known for going out much—and doing so on the night of my father's murder could easily be construed as suspicious. And I dug up dirt on both of them, just in case I needed blackmail.

I bought a knife and a whetstone. For the better part of a week, I worked on the blade, sharpening it until it could cut a tomato just by touching the skin. I bought vacuum-sealed coveralls, a hairnet, and a balaclava, all from different stores on different occasions, using cash.

After that, finding the perfect moment to strike was simply a matter of securing my alibi. One day, Josh showed me a picture of his girlfriend back home, gushing about how beautiful she was. And I remembered his breakup with his last girlfriend—how he'd kicked her out of his car and abandoned her on the side of the road in the middle of nowhere because a friend texted him proof that she'd been cheating on him.

He could be relied on to do it again.

So I asked him about his new girl—Gloria. He said he

trusted her and went on about how different she was from the one who broke his heart. I asked him what he would do if he found out for a fact that she was cheating. He said he'd leave, of course. He wouldn't stand around for an explanation. He'd just turn around and never speak to her again.

I was already a whiz with Photoshop. So I popped over to Green Bay and followed the girl around for a day until I had enough good photos to plug into the program and create the "proof" to convince Josh she was cheating. The pictures were my alibi—a dog whistle to get him back home exactly when I needed him.

Midterms ended on a Thursday, and Mikey flew out that very night, leaving his junker parked in our driveway. Josh left for Green Bay the next day—four hours and fifteen minutes away from our little house in Chicago by bus. I checked the bus schedule and scheduled my message to give him just enough time to break up with his girlfriend and get to the station to take the last bus back home.

Timing was everything.

When I arrived at my childhood home in Onalaska, I'd been sick to my stomach. Nervous, excited, struggling to believe I was actually there with a knife in my hand.

I slipped in through the back door. My father would be asleep. He'd always been an early-to-bed, early-to-rise kind of guy. In fact, as I made my way up the stairs—skipping the ones that creaked—I could hear his loud, burbling snore.

It was fifteen minutes after eight. I remembered because I glanced at the old-school digital alarm clock next to his bed. While he slept, I set up a tripod with the camera I'd borrowed from Josh—I knew better than to bring along my phone—and started recording. Just like Justin would've done.

Over the years, I rewatched the video enough times to memorize every detail of my kill.

"Hi, Justin," I stage-whispered to the lens, pulling down my mask to show my face. "My name is Erik Waller, and this is my father, the only so-called family I have in the world."

My father snorted and shifted in his sheets, freezing the blood in my veins. I glanced over my shoulder, waiting for him to settle before turning back to the camera. The thought of Justin seeing me flinch made me so angry that I cut the recording and started over.

I spoke more clearly the second time. "You said you wanted proof that I'm ready to be a part of your family." I looked back at the old man and drew the nine-inch blade from my duffel bag. "Are you ready?"

After securing the balaclava over my nose, I moved to my father's king-size bed. He always slept curled up on the side of the bed nearest the door, the other side empty where my mother used to be. The void that nobody could fill. He loved that invisible corpse so much more than me.

Rage flooded my body, followed by an unfamiliar sense of elation. At last, after all these years, he'd finally get what he deserved.

"Dad?" I spoke louder, and he began to stir. He knew it was me, even if he never got a chance to flip over and look.

The memory was a blur. A smear.

Sometimes, all I saw was the aftermath—me standing there, panting, looking down at what used to be my father. His face, neck, chest—just pulp and blood and gaping holes. A canvas of rage.

Other times, it was too clear.

The hot spray hitting my cheeks. The way he choked when the blade entered his windpipe. The scream that cut off halfway through. The *pop* of cartilage giving way. My shoulder aching from swinging again and again, the blade dulling but my arm not stopping. I couldn't stop. Not until I was sure.

When it finally ended—when there was nothing left in him to kill—I backed away, dripping and shaking and high as hell on adrenaline.

I grabbed the camera. Bagged the knife. My clothes were soaked. I stripped down in the en suite bathroom—a room he never let me enter, not even once.

That made it feel right, somehow. Like justice. Like invasion.

The shower scalded my skin, but I barely noticed. I scrubbed and scrubbed until the water ran pink instead of red before stepping into a fresh pair of coveralls, gloves, and cheap, untraceable tennis shoes.

Before I left, I shattered the back door window with my elbow—just enough to sell the break-in story.

On the drive home, I dumped the trash bag and the blade in a dumpster I'd tracked for weeks. Pick-up was scheduled for morning. By the time anyone found his body, the evidence would be halfway to a landfill in Michigan.

When I got back home, I snatched up the remote and turned on the TV. When I was sure I'd covered all my bases, I fell onto the couch, pulled a blanket up to my chin, and faked sleep. I'd been doing that for a month, pretending shit was broken with my system in my bedroom.

The door opened gently. I listened as Josh plodded inside. He stepped into the kitchen and opened the fridge before his footfalls approached. When he paused, I knew he was looking at me. And that was all he had to do—see me there asleep, quiet, not murdering anybody.

The rush I got from that—from so expertly predicting and manipulating his behavior—was almost as powerful as the feeling that came from stabbing the knife into my father's worthless flesh.

Joshua switched off the TV and dragged himself to his bedroom, shutting and locking the door behind him. That was when I heard him crying. But after that, I slept like a baby, secure in the knowledge that the old bastard was finally dead. I knew I'd been *careful and that even if the cops suspected me, they'd never be able to pin anything down.*

And I'd been right about that.

But I'd been wrong about Justin Black. I thought he was like me, looking for a family. I'd trusted him. Never again would I make that mistake.

Everything was different after that night. I didn't care about Justin anymore. In fact, I wouldn't have let him join my family if he got down on his knees and begged with an open mouth. He didn't matter. The day was coming when I'd be able to show him just how little I cared. He was just an old NPC who'd played his part. Now it was time for me to step up and finish the damn job.

My head lolled forward, and I barely had the energy to move it back against the wall.

Maybe three pink pills was too many.

I scanned the room until my gaze landed on Manoj, and I grimaced in disgust. I had looked for so long and so carefully to find my very own Timothy Stewart. I'd thought Manoj would fill the role perfectly—bad attitude, rebellious, lying to his family, stealing from his work. Stronger than he looked, but still beta AF and easy to manipulate.

Manoj was a tightly wound ball of impotent teenage rage. I'd thought that by giving him a chance to expel some of his simmering hatred, he'd be grateful.

It was time for me to face facts and admit I was wrong. The stupid jackass was too stubborn to accept the opportunity I laid so generously at his feet. Maybe Justin was onto something, picking someone so young to be his protégé. What Tim Stewart had lacked in strength, he'd more than made up for with blind admiration. That was what I needed.

I smiled for the first time in a long while as a memory bubbled to the surface from all the time I'd spent spying on

Manoj and his little family through a Wi-Fi camera I'd installed outside their house. I knew a way not only to get myself a better protégé, but to get the most out of Manoj while I still had him. It was all so simple.

Killing two birds with one stone was easy. All I had to do was lock them in a cage first. The kid would never even know what hit him.

13

After dropping Noah and Ariel off at the office to get to work fact-checking Joshua Sutherland's story, Winter drove down to the precinct to meet with Darnell on her own. No one was in the mood to go home and go to bed with a nineteen-year-old kid missing.

What little information Darnell already provided had her spiraling. Maybe Ariel was right that she was getting tunnel vision, because the only suspect in her mind was Erik Waller. He'd gotten fed up with Lessner for whatever reason or felt like he was starting to lose control of him...so he killed him.

And what was this newest move all about? Taking a kid? She guessed it was more than to get her attention. Having just killed Lessner, his latest protégé, Erik needed someone else to do his dirty work. But someone so young? And kidnapping? That was a Justin move if she ever saw one.

Under normal circumstances, Winter would've been bothered that she was clearly falling into the investigative trap of believing her own theories to the exclusion of objective truth. She was hunting for evidence to support the narrative already constructed in her head.

In her defense, she wasn't working this case as an investigator. She wasn't an FBI agent or a cop, and nobody was paying her as a private detective. She was a victim desperately searching for a way to protect herself and her family. She really didn't give a damn about using proper techniques or giving anybody alive the benefit of the doubt. All she wanted was Erik Waller.

And she wanted him dead, if she was being honest.

As she stepped into Detective Darnell Davenport's office, he shut the door behind her. Though never bright-eyed nor bushy-tailed, Darnell was looking rougher than usual. It was late, though. His brown eyes were weighed down with gray bags, and both his chin and head sported a heavy shadow. His suit hadn't been pressed properly, and he'd poorly knotted his tie. The lines between his eyebrows were deeper than usual, as were the furrows on his forehead.

Clearly, Harlan Lessner's treachery had hit him hard. Having worked alongside the man for years, Darnell had to be questioning his own instincts and skills as an investigator for not noticing when Lessner went dirty. Besides that, Winter had no doubt Darnell blamed himself for letting Lessner escape. If their roles were reversed, Winter would've been tearing herself to pieces.

"Lessner was shot six times. Twice in the gut and four times in the chest." Darnell sat beside her, choosing the chair on the window-facing side of his desk. The lighting in his office seemed to deepen his wrinkles and made his skin ashier. "He died instantly, but the body was left bleeding out for some time before it was loaded into the trunk of a '93 Ford Escort."

Winter pressed a hand over her mouth and closed her eyes. She thought again of the children she'd seen playing with the foam blocks at Sutherland's workplace, the softness in her husband's voice as he talked about bugs.

Lessner the man was neglectful, misguided, and selfish, but Lessner the father was devoted to his deceased daughter. Winter would never forget feeling his pain when he explained why he did what he did. Why he worked with Erik. It was all for the memory of his daughter and to make right the wrong done against her.

Harlan Lessner had fallen victim to a classic mistake—in fighting monsters, he himself had become one. After all, he was the one who, at Erik's behest, had hit Noah with his car, kidnapped him, and cut off one of his fingers. He was the one who strangled Eve until she passed out and beat her head against the ground until it bled. He'd nearly done the same to Winter.

Yet Winter couldn't help but feel an electric twinge of empathy. Most "evil" people ended up that way because of the wrongdoings that had befallen them. Her own little brother fit that mold.

Because Winter knew exactly how much Justin suffered, she'd given him one chance after another, so many more than he deserved, until she realized the suffering child was already dead, killed by the monster who replaced him.

Lessner had undergone a similar transformation. It never failed to break her heart to see a good person fall so far and hit so hard.

Winter didn't have kids, but she knew what it meant to love someone. If she had a daughter and somebody killed her with their recklessness, lied about it, and got off with a little slap on the wrist, what might she have done?

Shuddering, she turned away from Darnell and gazed out the window at the starless sky. She'd fought so many monsters in her life, each time barely escaping turning into one herself. Would Erik be the one to finally push her over the edge?

The day she found Noah strapped to a ticking bomb had

filled her with such wild anger. She knew for a fact that if Erik had come strolling out as she sat in the dirt cradling the battered body of her husband, she'd have shot him. Even if he was unarmed. Even if he was ready to cooperate. She'd have shot him right in the heart and felt nothing but vindication as she watched him fall.

Winter swallowed the lump in her throat, praying it wouldn't come to that. Hating the path her mind continued to tread, she shook her head and forced herself to refocus. "Was it the car he stole after breaking free of the prison transport?"

"No. The car belongs to a teenager named Manoj Bakshi. His mother, Jaya Bakshi, reported him missing this morning."

"Erik Waller."

"We're in agreement. The odds of Lessner running to his only ally are through the roof. And it seems it got him killed. If Manoj Bakshi left his car on the side of the road, he wouldn't have likely left the keys in it. It's a stretch to imagine Manoj abandoned it and then Erik stumbled on it and used it to deliver Lessner's body to our door. No, this feels like a pointed message." Darnell rested both elbows on his knees. "Have you heard any more from him?"

She shook her head. "He's overdue."

"Why do you think he did it?"

"Why do birds fly? Why do fish swim? This is just what he does. He finds broken, traumatized people with an axe to grind, whips them into a frenzy, and sends them out to do his dirty work. Once they've either lived out their usefulness or they start to rebel, he kills them."

Darnell blinked slowly. Having seen so many secrets buzz around his eyes in the past, she could tell he was weighing whether to tell her something. "Everybody in the precinct is currently obsessed with this case."

"I can't imagine why." Winter crossed her legs. "I'm not complaining."

"Our blood-spatter tech had a look at the body. He noticed droplets on Lessner's pants that were inconsistent with his injuries. He took a sample of the spatter and ran a blood type analysis. Results came back just a few minutes ago. It wasn't Lessner's blood."

Winter sat bolt upright and scooched forward in her chair. "Erik's? He's injured?"

"Don't look so happy about it."

"If he's injured, that'd put him off his game. He'll start making stupid mistakes."

"Well, this was certainly intentional. Had a damn BOLO out on a vehicle that'd been parked in our lot all day." Darnell showed a broken smile. "DNA analysis is in the works. I expect the results to be in very soon. Tomorrow, hopefully early, given the owner of the car has reported her teenage son missing. We also found gunshot residue on his hands."

"On Lessner's?" Her heart fluttered in her chest. "That means he shot Erik."

"Maybe." He gave his head a slow, wary shake. "I think after Lessner escaped, he and Erik came together at a predetermined meeting spot. Then they got into an argument. Shots were fired, and Erik came out on top. But I don't think Lessner went down without a fight."

"Attaboy, Lessner." Winter's hand went to her neck, her fingers gently pressing into the bruises Lessner left when he nearly strangled her too. "The driver of the car…does he have a record? Maybe a deep, dark secret you managed to uncover?"

"Background is clean as a whistle. The kid's never so much as shoplifted. Has a good relationship with Mom, according to her. No reason to think he'd run away. Holds down a job to help pay bills at home." Darnell shook his head.

Winter knew that look of defeat well. "If Erik hasn't kidnapped him to be his next crony, then the kid's probably…" She didn't want to finish.

"Already dead."

Yep.

Her body was like a windup toy with the key already turned as far as it would go. For as exhausted as she must've looked, she felt like a ball of energy ready to explode. "Can I have Jaya Bakshi's contact information?"

Darnell gave her a long side-eye followed by an even longer sigh. "Why not? You'll just look it up anyway." Snatching up one of his cards and a pen, he copied down some information from his computer screen and held it out to her. "Tomorrow. Don't go knocking on her door tonight, Black."

Winter almost smiled at that. "Understood." She gave him a look and reached for the card, but when she tried to pull it away, he didn't let go.

"You have to call me if you find anything."

"I promise."

"Even if it seems insignificant. You understand? You have to call me. Immediately."

Winter batted her lashes innocently. "Would I ever leave you out of the loop?"

His stony expression gave nothing away. "I don't find anything about you even remotely funny."

"I know." She yanked the card out of his grasp. "The feeling's mutual."

14

After breakfast with Noah and her grandparents the next morning, Winter drove to the other side of town to the small, single-story ranch house where Manoj Bakshi lived with his mother, grandfather, and younger brother. She killed the ignition and put the vehicle in park, taking out her phone to call Ariel.

Before she could even unlock the screen, it rang.

She swiped to answer the call. "Great minds think alike. Do you have any new information for me?"

"Yeah, I do." Ariel sounded strange, either like she'd been crying or like she'd just spent the whole day at an amusement park screaming and lost her voice. "I just got off the phone with Joshua Sutherland's ex. Gloria Allen."

"Are you okay?"

"Mm-hmm." She cleared her throat. "She got really mad when I brought the whole thing up and kinda yelled at me. And swore at me. She called me a liar and a parasite."

"What? Why?"

"Well, according to her, she never cheated on him. She never even met anybody named Ernst Zippler. She says the pictures were all faked to try to get Sutherland to break up with her. And then her whole friend group started treating her badly because they also thought she was a cheater. And then she kinda blamed me for ruining her reputation, her social circle, and the last few months of her life."

"Do you think she was telling the truth?"

"Well, I wasn't sure. You know people get really defensive when they're trying to cover something up. But then I found Zippler."

"Who is he? Did you speak to him?"

"I separated out his image from the one Gloria Allen sent to me. I did a reverse lookup, which took me to his Instagram. His real name is Tyler Cochran, and he's a male model."

Winter nibbled on her bottom lip. "Gloria Allen was telling the truth."

"It looks that way. I still think Sutherland dodged a bullet, though. She's not very nice."

"Great work, Ariel. Honestly, you're awesome." Winter popped open the SUV door and swung her leg out. "I'm here to talk to the family of the man who drove the car Harlan Lessner's body was found in. I'll text to check in when I'm done. Talk to you soon."

Hanging up, she slipped the phone into her pocket and passed through a garden of tulips and fragrant hyacinths, following an adorable cobblestone path to a pastel blue door. She rang the bell and waited.

A moment later, the dead bolt clunked open, and a petite woman opened the door. Her long black hair was pulled into a bun, a floral shawl over her shoulders. It was hard to say how old she was, since her face was puffy from crying and her wrinkles seemed deepened from stress.

She didn't say a word.

"I'm sorry to disturb you. My name's Winter Black-

Dalton. I'm a private investigator working with the Austin PD. I'm following up, and I was hoping I could speak with you about Manoj?"

The woman stood frozen, her lips slightly parted. "What?"

Winter fetched out her credentials and showed them to her. "May I ask your name, please, ma'am?"

Her jaw trembled and she cleared her throat. "Jaya Bakshi. Manoj is my son. Have you found him?" Her accent lay somewhere vaguely between Indian subcontinent and posh British, so light it barely brushed the edges of her vowels.

"Have you been informed that his car was found?"

She nodded, her expression hardening. "And a body in the trunk, but not his. Yes, the detective that was here earlier told me."

"I'm afraid there haven't been any further developments. May I come in and ask you a few questions, though, Mrs. Bakshi?"

"Of course." Jaya took a step back to hold the door open for Winter. "Please, take off your shoes. And you may call me Jaya."

Winter did as she was asked, leaving her boots on the porch, before following Jaya to a small living room. Inviting Winter to take a seat, Jaya went to the kitchen and brought her a glass of water.

"Thank you." Winter smiled politely and took a sip, pulling out her phone to take notes. "You might've answered some of these questions already, but please, bear with me. May I ask who all lives in the household?"

"This is my father's home. When my husband passed eight years ago, my two sons and I moved here to be with him."

"What's your father's name?"

"Rahul Gupta."

"Is he home?"

Jaya shook her head. "No. He's at the senior center playing pickleball."

"What's your other son's name?"

"Hari."

"How old's Hari?"

"Ten. He's in school right now."

"How long was Manoj missing before you reported him?"

"He was closing at the market where he works. He usually gets home late, past my bedtime, so I didn't notice he hadn't come home until about eight the next morning. Yesterday."

"What's the name of the market where he works?"

"Black Cherry. He always came right home after closing, though. Always. And when I called him, and he didn't answer, I called the police right away."

Winter set her water down on the glass coffee table. "Did you think Manoj might've left on his own?"

Jaya shifted in her seat, her fingers fiddling with the tassels on her shawl. "Manoj and my father do not always see eye to eye. My father is a very traditional man. Manoj can be disrespectful at times and very hardheaded. In their arguments, Manoj has threatened to leave. But that was only ever said in anger. And as I said, he would never leave me and his brother to worry for him like this."

Winter decided not to probe any deeper into the relationship between Manoj and his grandfather. She could see how delicate the subject was, and the last thing she wanted was for Jaya to shut down. Besides, it didn't matter. She knew Erik had taken Manoj. She could feel it in her bones. Not to mention, Lessner was found in Manoj Bakshi's car. Full-on Erik Waller move, all ego.

Ariel's comment about tunnel vision buzzed through her brain. Winter swatted it away like a fly. "Tell me more about Manoj. Does he have any close friends? A girlfriend?"

Jaya shook her head. "Manoj has always kept to himself. When he does make friends, he has a bad habit of burning bridges the moment there is the slightest disagreement. My son is incredibly stubborn and has never listened to a single word of advice anyone has ever given him."

Hearing more about Manoj's temperament, Winter began to understand what Erik might've seen in him. Which greatly bolstered the chances that he hadn't killed him. Yet.

"At the same time, he is loyal to this family." Jaya's eyes brimmed with tears. "He works to contribute to the household. And he loves his little brother." She brushed her hands against her eyes.

Winter pulled a tissue from a box next to her and pressed it into the woman's trembling hand. "Take your time."

"Tell me the truth, please." Jaya squared her slight shoulders. "Do you know what has happened to my son? The detective…he was respectful, but both times he was here, he told me nothing. Not really."

Winter hesitated. Whatever details the police chose to withhold, there was good reason for it. But she also didn't want to leave the poor woman twisting in the wind. "I believe your son was kidnapped."

Jaya's eyes tightened, wetness clinging to the surface again. She placed her long thin fingers over her frowning lips.

"The only comfort I can give is that the man I believe took him is a known offender. The police, the FBI, and I are all looking for him." Winter wished she could give more. She always did. But empty promises were worse than rubbing lemon juice and salt into a wound.

"Manoj has asthma." Jaya's voice warbled with fear and heartbreak. "He needs his control inhaler daily. I don't want to think what might happen—"

"Did he have his medication with him?"

She raked her fingernails through her hair, her composure cracking. "His rescue inhaler is always in his pocket, but if someone takes it from him…"

Jaya didn't need to tell her more. Manoj had to be found. Now. The stress of the situation could trigger a very nasty attack. One he might night have his inhaler for. That was if Erik left him alive at all.

What the hell does Erik want with this kid?

It was up to Winter to find out.

15

Back at the offices of Black Investigations, Winter sat down at her desk and began the filthy task of combing through the message boards on Justin's fan site. Using the Wayback Machine, an extensive internet archive of more than nine hundred billion web pages, she was able to not only locate several fan sites but look up comments by username.

What Ariel confirmed about Gloria Allen and Ernst Zippler lent credence to everything Joshua Sutherland had told them, and the username he provided for Erik—Juswinterik—proved to be authentic and active. The post history was a textbook example of a toxic parasocial relationship.

Using the date of posted comments to guide her, Winter followed Erik's online movements. Over the course of last year, he'd started out by watching all of Justin's archived videos, which included torture, murder, and a hell of a lot of psychopathic grandstanding. She didn't have to watch any of those videos to see the comment section, though—and the thumbnails alone were enough to pull the taste of vomit into the back of her throat.

Ever since Noah raided Carl Gardner's offices and confirmed her stalker was connected to Justin's fan community, Winter had been plagued by the sickly feeling of tiny spiders crawling up and down her spine. She hadn't slept peacefully a single night since.

She'd known, of course, that Justin had fans. They weren't simply going to disappear because he was convicted and serving several life sentences. If anything, it would encourage their love for him and inspire others to want to step up and fill his empty shoes.

A Justin Black copycat was horrifying enough, but Erik Waller was more than that. As she read Juswinterik's comments, a horrible suspicion settled on her shoulders. Somehow, even behind the layers of locked gates and doors, Justin was still communicating with the outside world.

Erik had left hundreds of comments, each more hateful than the last. Her eyes began to glaze over, her brain teetering on the edge of dissociation. Time and again, he gushed over Justin's atrocities, salivating over the most horrible sins one human could commit against another.

Winter's bones began to ache, and her shoulders hunched, like she had the beginnings of a cold coming on. Her brain and heart sapped energy from every limb to steel her against the onslaught of memories—Justin taunting her, torturing her, forcing her to bear witness. With shallow breaths, she waited for the deluge of emotions to overtake her. But her memories stayed in the past where they belonged, thankfully.

When she came upon Erik's response to the video of the day Timothy Stewart's family were all killed, she had to stop a moment to look away. Of all the nightmares that plagued her and the memories she wished she could forget, no others were as strong or insistent. Her hands tingled like the stab of a thousand needles. The same hands she'd used when Justin forced her to murder two innocent parents while their son looked on.

Erik's comment under this video was uncharacteristically brief. *Your sister is a snaaaaaaack!!!*

Winter froze. Her stomach turned, and she groaned deep in her throat. "This just gets better and better."

"Winter?"

"What?" She jerked at Ariel's voice before wiping a hand over her eyes and taking a steadying breath. "What's up?"

"We have a couple new summons requests here that need to be taken down to the courthouse today."

"Okay. Come right back when you're done."

Ariel's eyes widened like those of a frightened puppy. "You want me to take them?"

Winter slapped her forehead before she could stop the reaction. "What else would I want you to do? Flush them down the toilet?"

"Okay." Ariel clenched her teeth and stuck her chin out. "What the hell?"

"I'm so sorry." Winter massaged her temples, fighting back the tears burning a path through her sinuses. "It's this fucking case. I think I'm going crazy."

"I know." Ariel's voice softened. "But you're not. And we're going to find him. I know we will."

Winter nodded, her tongue planted hard in her cheek. She'd already used up all her cockeyed optimism last week when Noah was kidnapped, having no choice but to believe she would find him and bring him back safe or go completely mental.

Her reserves were utterly depleted.

"I'll just go drop these off. I'll be right back."

"Thank you." Winter waited for Ariel to exit before she turned back to the execrable words on her screen.

Erik's comments began to revolve more and more around

her after that initial one. He wrote graphic descriptions of what he wanted to do to her, most of which included killing her or getting her pregnant—or both. She found a short fan fiction just a couple of paragraphs long in which he described the way he wanted to kill Noah, including slicing off his ring finger and taking his wedding band.

Any doubt still lingering that Juswinterik could be anyone other than Erik melted away.

She didn't know Justin's username, so it was a slow process, reading all the comments and trying to find anything that Justin might say. But Juswinterik's posts were not like the others. Rather than talking to the masses and going back and forth with other fans, it was like he was writing directly to Justin. For nearly a year, even as Winter and her team back in Richmond were hunting Justin down, he'd written to her brother. Just to him.

Neither of us ever had a family. People we could actually depend on instead of these worthless losers we're both related to. You tried to build a new family with Timothy and Winter, but they weren't ready to accept the truth. I'm ready to be your family.

Only one other person had responded to that post, two months into Justin's permanent solitary confinement. Username Jb695.

Prove it, bitch.

Justin. It had to be.

Fury sizzled through Winter's blood at the thought. Justin was far too dangerous to be allowed access to the internet. How the hell could he be getting away with this?

The only possible explanation was that Justin had set up some kind of arrangement with one or more of the prison guards. It wouldn't have been the first time he'd manipulated privileges and favors out of people who were supposed to be on the side of law and order. Would he have been able to charm a guard with nothing but smiles and persuasive words, or was it possible Justin's fans were willing to pay well for access to their false idol?

An even worse thought occurred to her. What if one of his guards was also a fan?

If she was right about Jb695, the timeline put Erik's first contact with Justin five weeks before Benjamin Waller was murdered.

Prove it, bitch.

There was one person who might yet be able to point her in the right direction. The only person other than Erik Waller who might know exactly what happened to his father and the truth about Erik's endgame.

A soft rapping on the door announced Noah. "Manoj Bakshi's market, Black Cherry, has security cameras in the store. The owner showed me footage of Erik, dressed just like he was in the park, in a brown wig with extra-thick boots and layers to beef him up. It was him, plain as a fly on the wall. Eating lunch in there, day after day. They all recognized him, and the APD had been there before me, so they know that he was…" He cut himself short. "What's wrong?"

"What? Me? Nothing."

"Then why have you got that face on?"

Winter tried to force an easy expression, but it was too much work. "I need to go to New Mexico."

"New Mexico?"

She hesitated. Justin's location was secret, and she wasn't even sure she could make enough phone calls to convince anyone to let her see her brother—but she had to try, and she needed Noah's support.

The penny seemed to drop for Noah. "Is that where he is?" His muscles tightened one by one. "That's a bad idea."

"Not if we're going to catch Erik before he kills again."

Noah grunted and folded his arms. "All you're going to

get from your brother is lies and riddles, like always. If he's been working with Erik, do you really think he'll give it up so easily?"

"Do you have a better idea?"

Noah snarled at the floor and ground his teeth. "I'm coming with you."

"He won't talk if you're there."

"I go where you go."

"Justin doesn't like you."

The skin under one green eye twitched. "It's mutual."

Winter cracked her neck. "You can come. That's if they'll even let me go. But if they do…I need you to come. I can't…I mean, I don't want to do this without you."

"I'm there, darlin'. You try and stop me."

"But you have to promise to behave. We won't get anything out of him if you lose your temper."

"Don't worry." Noah bared his teeth like a smiling wolf. "I don't bite."

16

Winter used her business credit card to purchase two plane tickets from Austin to Albuquerque. Arriving well after visiting hours, she and Noah found a small hotel and ordered in takeout. After thoroughly barricading the door just in case, they took matching couples' doses of melatonin and went to sleep.

Tossing and turning in sweaty sheets, Winter ruminated on memories and worries about the day ahead. Every moment she had to wait felt like an eternity, and she was consumed by a sense of dread as the minutes ticked by. She and Noah rose early and got out on the road in their rental car, heading through the desert toward the undisclosed location of ADX Valdez—one of America's only supermax prisons.

Winter had been there once before, right after Justin was sentenced to spend the rest of his life in the facility. He'd escaped from a psych hospital the first time she caught him, taking her unconscious body along on his way out, so they'd needed to make sure the place was actually secure this go-round, for her own peace of mind.

Only a few dozen prisoners were housed in the facility. Many of them were leaders of gangs or cartels, so there was a high chance someone out in the world might try to help them escape. These violent criminals were like Justin, whose hordes of fans would've been outside the gate protesting every single day if they ever found out where it was.

To ensure that didn't happen, Noah and Winter followed a scripted route through checkpoints designed to ensure they weren't followed. She didn't want to imagine the consequences of Justin's fans finding out where he was being kept. They'd already proven they were willing to do anything. And some of them, including Erik Waller, had the money to follow through with it.

Each prisoner in the supermax lived in perpetual solitary confinement. There were no orange jumpsuits or gangs or dayrooms or time in the yard. Prisoners here never went outside or saw the sun. Save the watch tower and a small area for the guards, the entire facility was underground with a single elevator leading in and out.

The security was more intense than any she'd ever experienced. Just to come inside, she and Noah had to not only hand over all their IDs and credentials for scrutiny, they had to submit to full body scans and searches. They had to give up their weapons, their belts, their phones, and their wallets.

"He hasn't been very cooperative this morning, so we'll need a few more minutes." The guard who'd confiscated their personal items waved them toward an office. "You can wait in there."

Very hospitable.

As they sat in the cramped office, Winter finally told Noah the truth. "You can't come in with me."

His shoulders twitched just a little, though his face remained unchanged. "Oh?"

"I'm sorry, but we can't risk Justin clamming up." She pressed her hands on each side of his face in the hopes of softening the blow. "And I don't want to have to talk to him any longer than necessary."

"This is a bad idea." Noah's warning expression made it clear he was more worried than shocked. In fact, he already seemed resigned to the idea. "You sure you don't want me to just stand behind you and look scary?"

"Nobody can look scary in the background like you do, babe." Winter smoothed down the lapel of his brown leather jacket. "And that's exactly why you need to wait for me here."

"Ms. Black?" A guard held open the heavy metal door of the waiting room. "The prisoner's ready. I'll take you down."

Smiling politely, Winter nodded. Her hand lingered a moment on her husband's cheek. His worried expression snaked like an ice cube down her back, and she had to close her eyes to get herself to pull away from him.

"He's not your brother." Noah's words followed her just before the door swung shut, closing her in with the guard.

A metallic buzz sounded, followed by a click as the door locked behind her automatically. Every door in ADX Valdez was always locked, not just the cells. Most of them seemed to have at least two types of door—one connected to the central electrical system and another that was purely physical. To say she felt uneasy to be locked into one of the most inescapable prisons ever built by humans was a gross understatement.

With two guards in front of her and two behind, Winter followed down a shiny metal hall. They passed through no less than six security doors, each one comprising three layers of heavy metal and automatically sealing themselves just like the first one had.

Finally, they came to the elevator that would take them down to "the pit," as the guards called the cellblock floor.

Winter clenched her teeth and focused on breathing

evenly through her nose. She tried not to give any credence to the sweat on her palms, the insistent rattling of her teeth whenever she opened her mouth.

Though she had looked forward to never seeing Justin again as long as she lived, fate had other plans. She reminded herself of everything he'd done and would continue to do until she caught him. Only that gave her the strength she needed to keep putting one foot in front of the other.

He's not my brother, she thought again and again, just to make sure she wouldn't forget when she looked into his icy-blue eyes. *My brother is dead.*

Two guards remained at the top of the elevator, each inserting a key and entering a code, while Winter and the other two stepped inside. They inserted their own keys to open the pad, which housed only three glowing buttons. The guard pressed the one at the bottom and entered yet another code before the elevator groaned and began to sink.

She had no idea how deep in the earth the cells actually were. Too far to tunnel out in a lifetime.

When the doors swished open, a single long hallway stretched before her with a series of steel gates at the far end. Winter shivered away an encroaching sense of claustrophobia, or perhaps just a very rational fear of the place itself.

Tracks of abrasive fluorescent lighting cast long shadows behind each of the guards, cold light glowing on the concrete walls, floor, and ceiling. The whereabouts of each prisoner's cell were classified, and the inmates were frequently shifted around to cause even more confusion.

Winter had once seen a diagram of one of the cells at Valdez. It was very small, seven feet long by seven feet wide. No furniture, just a built-in bench for a bed, a toilet, and a sink. No personal possessions were permitted, and there were no windows.

It was difficult to imagine a more sterile existence. She wondered just how much Justin had withered, being locked away from the sun for eight months.

The guards led her to a metal door and instructed her to wait while they peeled back three layers of security. Her heart leaped into her throat, and she fought back an unwelcome sense of sympathy.

Justin deserved to be here, dammit.

He was guilty of everything he'd ever been accused of. He deserved to suffer for what he'd done. Last time she'd forgotten that, a lot of people ended up dead. She would never forget again.

As the guards pulled open the final door, they invited Winter to step inside. She'd already been warned not to touch the prisoner or give him anything and to stand back at least an arm's length at all times.

Before her was a wall of shiny steel bars woven in tight formation. Winter stepped inside, and the outer partition was closed behind her. Light buzzed from an overhead fixture. Justin sat directly in front of her on a stone slab, his hands cuffed and his feet in manacled together and a chain at his waist attached to the wall. Everything in the cell was white—cold and clinical—including the jumpsuit he was dressed in.

"Winter?" His eyes brightened, though they still looked gray in such cold light. "I was sure you were going to be somebody else."

"Who..." Her voice cracked, making the word barely audible. She tried again. "Who were you expecting?"

Justin's smile widened—that winning smile that had led so many to their deaths. "It doesn't matter. I'm much happier it's you. How did I get so lucky?"

She kept her back pressed against the outer door. It was

the only way to stay an arm's length back from the bars in such a small space. "I need to ask you some questions."

"What a coinkydink. I need to ask you some questions too. What have you been up to lately, Sissy Poo?"

She flinched internally at that horrible name, but she refused to let him see her unease. "I need to ask about one of your followers."

"Give me a break, Sissy. The very first time you come to visit me and all you wanna do is talk shop?" He stuck his bottom lip out. "I don't think so."

"Shop is all we have." She managed to keep her tone low and remarkably measured. "I hate you."

He giggled the way he used to whenever he had a bloody knife in his hand. Prison had already changed his looks—he was skinnier and grayer, and what had once been pearly whites were beginning to yellow. But that smile had more staying power than an irradiated cockroach.

"I heard you got married. I hope not to that same son of a bitch you were dating." He tilted his head back and forth and clucked his tongue. "That's a real shame. Noah is, like, so... whatever."

"I need you to answer my questions, Justin." Winter said his name because she knew he liked the sound of it, but it conjured a watery taste of pre-vomit under her tongue.

"What's in it for me, Sissy?" He shifted in his manacles, dragging one leg tightly over the other to cross them. Something about the gesture eased her enough to unclench her jaw. He was trying hard to look casual and in control, but he was so thoroughly subjugated, it just came off as ridiculous.

Winter wiped the crust from the corners of her lips. "What do you want?"

"I just want to know what you've been up to lately. I hope life hasn't been too boring without me."

She turned and paced three steps from one side wall to the other, rolling out the tension in her shoulders. Justin wanted to make her squirm, as usual. It filled her with an incredible sense of relaxation and calm. Like when she was rock climbing and paused on the side of a cliff just to take in the view. Her heightened sense of danger increased her confidence. She felt relaxed in a way she rarely did in so-called normal situations.

"I don't really think about you." She showed him an easy smile of her own. "And when I accidentally do, it's just to remember to be grateful that I'm on this side of the steel door and you're on the other."

The skin under his eyes tightened along with his smile. "You've never been a good liar."

"You wouldn't know the truth if someone hanged you with it. You only ever listen to what you want to hear. So let's save some time. What is it you want to hear, hmm?"

Justin leaned forward, as much as his shackles allowed. "What I want to hear is—"

"You want to know about my personal life, I assume." She let the silence stretch, calm and steady, like she had all day. Like this was just another day. "Well, let's see. I'm married to the love of my life. I've made good friends in my new city. We have a beautiful house with a full-on white picket fence and a porch swing. I sleep every night in a soft, comfy bed. I go wherever I want and do whatever I want, if you can believe it."

Justin licked his lips, the intensity of his stare probing her every word, every move.

She smiled, small and unbothered. "Every morning, I wake up free. I go where I want, do what I want. And most days, I spend my time hunting people like you and making damn sure they end up in cages."

The more his expression tightened, the looser her muscles grew. The more he glared, the more she smiled.

"Did you hear any of that? Or do you still think I'm lying?"

"You think of me." He growled, low and quiet, like something rotting behind a wall. "You never forget me. When you rock in that little porch swing, you think of the trees we used to climb…the way we scraped our knees and bled together. When you laugh with your new friends, you look too long, searching their eyes for mine."

Saliva dripped from his lower lip to trail down his chin. Winter watched in fascination as it dropped to the cement floor.

"And when you're lying in that soft, fluffy bed with the love of your life…" He leaned forward, just enough to pull the air tight between them. "Just before you spread your legs for him and let him shove his—"

"Actually," she cut him off before he could finish what was sure to be an explicit sentence, "there's another man in my life. I think you might know him."

"Oh, really?" He glanced away, feigning boredom, but he couldn't keep his gaze off her for long.

"His name's Erik Waller. You might know him better as Juswinterik."

Justin leaned back and put a hand to his chin, the other lifting along with it in the cuffs. "I hate to admit this, Sissy, but I don't really get out to meet new people these days."

She only wished that were true. "You're full of shit."

"Am I?"

"I know you've been getting online. You've got some kind of arrangement with your fan club."

"But you don't know how, do you? And that means you don't know how to stop me." He giggled like the lead clown at a circus. "I'll never tell. You call this a prison? Bitch, please. I'm everywhere right now."

"You like that, don't you? Having some connection to the outside world?"

He lifted a shoulder in a lazy shrug. "Who you talkin' to?"

"One phone call from me, and I can have every single one of your guards changed forever."

He seemed to laugh her off, but she'd seen the twitch. She knew the truth.

"Oh, Sissy. You're such a bad liar. They'd never give you that kind of authority. Most of your career was spent making horrible decisions that got lots of innocent people killed. Ain't that why they pushed you out and turned you into a low-rent private dick?"

Winter pressed her lips together and took a deep breath through her nose. "Those are the kinds of stories that'll help keep you entertained after I cut off your Wi-Fi."

His expression shifted in an instant. "What do you want to know, exactly?"

Winter didn't attempt to hide her superior smirk at his capitulation. "I'm sorry, was I unclear? Erik. Waller."

"I might remember one or two things. But I need some information in exchange."

She rolled her eyes. "Such as?"

"I want an update on my Timmy Kimmy Coo-Coo."

Winter shuddered internally at the affection with which he spoke about the child he had kidnapped, groomed, and systematically tortured while dragging him along on a murder tour through Europe. Justin even forced the child to dress in girl's clothes and change his name to be more appealing to him.

"Timothy," Winter corrected, "is healing with a family who loves him."

"Do you ever talk to him? Does he miss me?"

There was that watery vomit again. "I don't talk to him, but I can assure you the answer is no. He doesn't miss you. Nobody does."

"You miss me, Sissy Poo."

"Erik. Fucking. Waller."

He waved her off with a loose wrist. "Yeah, I know him. Just another sad little bitch trying to get a taste of the master."

"Tell me about it."

"Who's the last person you killed?"

Winter's teeth snapped like a horse champing a bit. Always the same thing with him. It was almost comical at this point.

She stood in dumbstruck awe of how her past self had managed to make excuses and hold out hope for this thoroughly evil creature for so long. What the hell had she been thinking? It was so obvious that Justin was beyond redemption.

Now that she didn't care about his trauma or his soul, she saw him for exactly what he was. A pathetic child, desperate for attention. Getting what she wanted out of him was going to be so easy, it almost didn't seem fair.

She liked that even better.

17

"You want to know about the last person I killed? What their name was, why I killed them, whether they suffered?" Winter called to mind an incident from a few weeks ago. "It was a woman. Jessica Huberth. Fashionable lady. Hourglass figure, killer hair, flawless makeup. She ran a cosmetics business. Only that was just a cover for her drug business."

Justin seemed pleased to hear this. "How'd you kill her?"

"With a gun. She was in my office. I'm sorry to say I ruined her makeup. The bullet sort of erased her face."

"It's so good to catch up." Justin smiled like a cat who'd just spotted his dinner. "All right, I'll tell you about Erik. But you're gonna have to help me out. I have so many devoted fans, you know."

Winter's stomach turned. How she wished he was lying about that.

"He wrote to you last year and asked to be a part of your family. Juswinterik. You told him to prove it."

"Oh." Justin conked himself on the head with his cuffed hands. Seeing how thoroughly contained he was by the cell, the cuffs and manacles seemed like overkill. She was grateful for them, though. "That guy. I remember that guy. Basic bitch."

"Why do you say that?" Winter crossed her arms and leaned back against the wall. God, it was cold in there. For a second, she almost felt sorry for Justin having to endure such cold, day in and day out.

Then she remembered that he deserved so much worse.

"Erik Waller is a basic bitch name too."

"Well, that's something you two have in common. Names don't get more basic than 'Justin Black.' You sound like a bank teller."

His eyes narrowed, only for a moment, but Winter felt a surge of victory.

He recovered quickly with a laugh—high-pitched and musical like a hyena on mescaline. "Erik's in love with you. Did you know that?"

"Like Neptune loved Medusa. What I don't understand is why."

"Go look in a mirror, Sissy Poo-Poo. You're a Disney adult's wet dream."

"A what adult?"

"Disney adult. You know, adults who like to pretend they never grew up and want to live their lives in a magic castle with fairies and shit?"

Winter's head slumped back and bonked the wall gently. "What the hell are you talking about? And why?"

"Snow White, dummy. You could play her on TV. Or you could've ten years ago. You're starting to get crow's-feet, honey. And those elevens are deep! I always said you scowl too much."

Winter smiled in a *kindly go screw yourself* way. First Ariel and now Justin. Fine, she wasn't a spring chicken anymore, but that didn't mean AARP invites were coming in the mail just yet.

"Why does Erik like Snow White?"

"What's not to like?"

"That's not an answer."

"Who wouldn't want to find a beautiful woman lying dead in the woods, bring her back to life, then carry her home and away from all her friends to do as they please with her?"

Winter cringed inwardly, fighting to keep her body language casual.

"I think his mommy had black hair and pale skin, like you. That kid has serious mommy issues. He never said anything about it, but I can spot mommy issues a mile away. I mean, daddy issues will turn a person into an alcoholic or drug addict, but mommy issues will turn a man into a genuine menace to society."

"It seems to me like you remember him pretty well."

"He had some follow-through. I'll give him that. Most of my so-called followers are too cowardly to hold their own knife, so they just want to live through those who are brave. But every now and then, you get one that makes it all worthwhile."

"Tell me about Erik's follow-through."

"He wanted to marry you and be my brother so we could all go off on a bloody bender together." Justin shook with peals of sudden laughter. "Can you imagine?"

"That's gonna be difficult with you locked in here."

"Tell me about it." His tone was like a colleague commiserating by the watercooler. "It was gross, Sissy. I felt like he was proposing to me. Sooooo not my type. Freaking nobody's type, amirite? Gross little incel shut-in freak-boy. I mean, look at him. And look at me. Look at you. He wants to be in our family? Are you kidding me?" Giggles cascaded over his body like soap suds. "As if I'd ever give anybody permission to marry you!"

"Your permission is meaningless."

"Ha!" Justin wiggled his brows, a hint of his old charisma shining through. "I almost told him to screw off right then. But then I thought, why not see how this plays out, hmm? What happens when a man with mommy and daddy issues can not only never have the girl of his dreams, but can't have the approval of his mentor either?" Justin set his hands on his chest proudly. "That's me, by the way. I'm the mentor. It's me."

"Congrats." Winter drummed her fingers on her elbow, waiting for him to continue.

"Well?" he hissed.

"Well what?"

"Aren't you gonna tell me what that fruity little nutcake's been up to?"

Winter grimaced. She wasn't about to give Justin the satisfaction of running down everything Erik Waller had done to her…or for her. The people he'd killed and vicariously gotten killed. His own father Benjamin, her Aunt Opal, Cybil Kerie, Harlan Lessner, and all the people who died at their hands—at Erik's behest. Not to mention the untold psychological and physical torture he'd inflicted on her and Noah and Ariel and Eve.

Justin called Erik *basic*, but the sad fact of the matter was that he was anything but. If Justin knew all the things Erik had done, including his expert manipulations, he wouldn't brush him off so easily. If only he knew, Justin would either see Erik as a worthy successor or a hated rival. More likely a bit of both.

"You're here asking me about him." Justin cracked his neck as he turned his gaze to the ceiling. "I assume that means his dad wasn't a one-off?"

Winter perked up.

His smiled widened like a snake drawing back its gaping

jaw. "Stabbed him to death in his sleep and filmed the whole thing for my amusement."

Heat prickled up her spine, spreading out like pins and needles across her back and neck. The red smear on Sutherland's camera lens. It had to be Benjamin Waller's blood. Erik had borrowed the camera so he could leave his phone at home to help back up his alibi. "You watched the footage?"

"Mm-hmm. He sent it straight to me. What a moment! I mean, it was the culmination of a lifetime of repression, but he was impressively gangster about the whole thing. Cold as a mother-effer."

There was one mystery solved once and for all, although having only Justin's word to go on meant they'd never get a conviction.

Not unless that video still exists somewhere. And if Erik sent it to Justin, it probably does.

Ariel's research had confirmed the housemates were simply pawns in Erik's game rather than willing parties. She wondered if the use of Mikey Swage's car and Joshua Sutherland's camera were simply a matter of convenience or if Erik planned to frame them if need be.

Framing them would have been pretty stupid, given that their only connection to Benjamin was Erik himself.

His father had been his first kill, so of course it was a bit clumsy and out of character for the monster he eventually became. She wondered why he spent so much time grooming others to do the work for him if he actually had the stomach for it.

The simple answer was that he enjoyed manipulating others at least as much—if not more—than the pleasure he got from a personal kill.

Not unlike Justin. Neither of them could resist pushing the boundaries of what they could get away with. That tendency had been a huge factor in Justin's capture. The same would be true with Erik.

"Do you still keep in contact with Erik?"

He stuck his tongue hard in his cheek. "Wouldn't you like to know?"

"Justin…"

"Winter." There it was at last—the award-winning, Hollywood-worthy, Justin Black smile that made everyone go weak at the knees and want to do anything in their power to please him. "I can tell Erik has made himself a big ole thorn in your side. Since I'm not there to dig into you myself, I suppose it'll have to do. I know I can trust him to do things the way I would want them done."

"So he is working for you?"

"Wouldn't. You. Like. To. Know?"

"Oh, shut up." She pinched the bridge of her nose. "For once, just shut up."

"I don't think so, Sissy Poo." He giggled again, more animal than human.

Winter laughed, too, under her breath and shook her head. How had she ever found a way to make excuses for him? Her mind flashed with memories where she caused herself and so many others suffering because she refused to see Justin for the creature he was. She remembered it, but she didn't understand it anymore. She was no longer the same person.

The memories themselves still hurt, but his cruel words had lost their sting. Justin could've been any delirious psychopath in a prison, and she'd have felt exactly the same. If this kind of perspective was what came with getting older, Winter was grateful for her bad hearing and every fine line on her face.

"Okay, Justin. Talk away." She pushed the button on the

wall—a signal to the guards that she was ready to leave. "I hope the shadows answer."

"You're not leaving already." It wasn't a question or a request. He was ordering her to stay.

She laughed at that too. "I'm already gone."

"Winter? Don't go…"

"Oh, Justin? One last thing. That story I told you about shooting Jessica Huberth in the face? Total fabrication. I never shot any cosmetics dealer. And you ate it up. Like I said, you wouldn't know the truth if someone hanged you with it."

As rage suffused Justin's features, Winter smiled brightly enough to light up the miserable cell. The makeup company CEO and drug dealer had indeed died from a gunshot wound in Winter's office, but the person pulling the trigger had been her ex-husband, Kyle Fobb.

When the door slammed behind her, relief coursed through her body. Perhaps she was riding a wave of adrenaline and perhaps she would feel it later, but in the moment, she felt nothing. He meant nothing.

If only for that reason, she was glad she'd come.

18

Hari Bakshi finished blowing up the final balloon in his surprise. Tossing it up in the air, he punched it so it bobbed across the room and settled in the pile with the others.

His *maata* had been so sad since Manoj went missing. Hari knew he had to do something to cheer her up. It seemed like years since he'd thrown a *Best Mom Ever* party. Sometimes, he forgot to tell her.

She needed to hear it now.

Snatching a roll of tape, Hari picked up the pile of pictures he'd drawn for her and went about posting them all over the walls. One picture was of Maata, Manoj, Dada, and himself all standing together and smiling. Another one showed a rainbow and a flock of ducks, which were his maata's favorite. Hari snatched up a colored pencil and drew a baseball cap on one of the ducks.

Maata loved baseball. They all did, especially Manoj. Hari drew a tiny orange *H* on the baseball cap for the Houston Astros, Manoj's favorite team. Maata liked the Rangers better, so it was always a big deal when they played each other. They'd all argue and shout and laugh. Every one of their games was an event in the Bakshi house.

Hari hoped Manoj would come home soon. He was missing the regular season. They even had tickets to a game in two weeks—Rangers at Astros. Manoj would never miss that. He hoped his big brother would be home safe soon.

Standing back to admire his work, Hari wondered if there was anything else he needed. He chewed his lip and put his hands on his hips. He had plenty of time. Maata was showing houses out of town and wouldn't be home until dinner.

Food. Every party needed food. The ten-year-old took off his headphones, his music fading from a blast into a dull roar deep in his ears, and stepped out into the hall, closing the door behind him.

He heard a strange noise—an unfamiliar male voice—but a few cops had been by the house lately, so Hari didn't think too much of it. Except that his dada was so old that with Manoj gone, Hari was kind of the man of the house. He needed to be there if the cops were talking to his dada, especially with Maata at work.

Hari marched into the kitchen—and stopped dead at the scene in front of him. The unfamiliar man wasn't a cop but a tall white guy with blond hair in plain clothes. He had a black brace wrapped around his leg and a pistol in his hand.

Dada sat at the table, the barrel of the gun pressed against his temple. Yellow and greenish bruises encircled one eye, and blood trickled from a nostril. His thin body was folded in on itself and trembling.

Dada's glassy eyes snapped to Hari, suddenly clearer than he'd ever seen them.

"*Bhaag jao!*" he hissed under his breath. *Go away!*

It took longer than it should've for Hari to understand.

His gaze flinched between the gun and his shaking grandfather.

"I wouldn't do that if I were you." The man with the gun had a smile so caustic it could eat through walls. "If you run away, I'll kill your grandpa here, and it'll be your fault."

"Get away from him!" Hari shrieked.

The man's smile cooled a little as he tilted his head. The lump in his neck bobbed up and down as he breathed. "So you're Minage's little brother? I see it. Both of you haters too stubborn for your own good."

"Manoj?" Hearing his brother's name in the man's voice was an insult. "What did you do to my brother?"

"Don't stress about that. You've got more important stuff to worry about. Like whether I'm gonna kill this old man right here."

"Don't hurt him!" Hari lurched closer. Tears nipped at the corners of his eyes, but he refused to let them fall.

"That's up to you, little dude."

"What do you mean?"

"You like games, right? I got one for you." With his free hand, the man gestured Hari closer. "Come over here. I'll show you how to play. It's called Find the Lady."

Dada shook his head. "*Vah jhootha hai*. Don't—"

"Shut up, Unc. Damn." The man lifted his pistol and hit Dada in the back of the head, nearly sending him toppling off his chair.

Hari lifted a hand and staggered closer. "Stop it! Leave him alone!"

"All you have to do is find the lady. Pick the right card, I'll leave and never come back. Shit, I'll even let Manoj go." He smirked and pointed to three playing cards displayed in a row on the table. "Are you ready to play?"

Looking at his dada's blood, Hari saw no option but to do

as he was told. He went to the table and glared at the red backs of the playing cards.

Cold sweat beaded on his brow. He looked at his dada, who seemed to be slipping out of consciousness. "What happens if I pick wrong?"

"Oh, don't pick wrong. Don't do that."

His lips and fingers trembled, his heartbeat ramping up, fluttering like a bee's wings. Everything he knew about cards he'd learned from Manoj. He remembered the day Dada had caught them playing poker with candy for chips. Their grandfather had gotten so angry, he threatened to throw Manoj out of the house for trying to corrupt his little brother, and then the two of them spent the night arguing.

Hari used to think listening to his grandfather and brother shout at each other was the worst thing that could ever happen. He'd have given anything to go back and listen to one of their screaming matches now.

"One in three are good odds," Manoj said from deep in Hari's memory. *"I'd bet my life on those odds."*

The words had sounded both wise and hollow at the time. Now they made Hari want to throw up. It was one thing to bet his own life, but what about gambling with somebody else's?

"C'mon. I ain't got all day, kid. You've got five seconds to pick, or I'll just shoot you both on principle. M'kay?" The blond man lifted his eyebrows high, wrinkling his forehead and widening his eyes. "Five…"

Hari flinched and looked at the cards. They all looked the same.

"Four."

"Why are you doing this?"

"Three."

"We never did anything to you!" The tears he'd been

holding back leaked freely down his stinging cheeks. "Please. Just leave us alone."

"Two." The man tapped his gun against Dada's head.

"Fine!" Hari slapped the middle card and flipped it over. Joker.

"Ooh. Bad luck."

"Wait!" Hari turned and threw his hand in the air, but not before the blast of the gun went off. Screaming, Hari covered his ears and dropped to his knees. Something hot sprayed his face and arms.

Blood. His grandfather's blood.

With the shot still ringing in his ears, Hari barely heard the thump of the body falling to the floor.

Dada. No, it couldn't be true. He had to be having a nightmare. Things like this didn't actually happen. Eyes clenched shut, he coiled his body into a tight ball and ordered himself to wake up.

Sneakers squeaked in puddles of blood as the man slowly stepped closer. Then he crouched in front of Hari, his elbows resting on his knees, the gun loose in his hand. "Look at me."

Hari shook his head, clenching his eyes shut so tight it hurt.

This wasn't happening. It wasn't real. This couldn't be real.

"Look at me, or I'll fucking kill you!"

Hari flinched and opened his eyes, but he still couldn't see the man's face. All he could focus on was his grandfather lying flat on the kitchen floor with blood leaking from a big hole in the back of his head.

"Dada, no. You killed him. You killed him! Dada!"

The man slapped him across the face so hard that he fell to his back. His hands instinctively went up to protect himself from the next blow.

"Shut up."

Something hot touched Hari's temple—the gun. The gun that killed his dada. His crying doubled down. He tried to beg for his life, but nothing came out that made any sense. Only snot, tears, and nonsense.

This was it. He was about to die.

All he could think about was his maata. Would she come home and find them like this—her whole family murdered? She always said that if anything ever happened to him or Manoj, she would die a thousand deaths. If the man were still there when she got home, she'd probably throw herself at him and scratch his eyes out before a bullet ended her life.

He couldn't bear it. "Don't hurt my maata. Please. I'll do anything."

The man smiled cruelly, his dark eyes lifeless as a gray sky in winter. "That's more like it."

19

Winter and Noah had driven straight to the airport from ADX Valdez and managed to get on an earlier flight back to Austin. Every night they were away was a night her grandparents had no one to watch over them.

On the way into the city, they stopped home to pick up a few things before continuing to Winter's grandparents' house. Everything in her just wanted to stay and sleep in her own bed next to her husband and pretend everything was normal, but she couldn't justify it, knowing the only family she had left would be unprotected.

During their stint away, Winter had low-key annoyed her grandparents, calling them every hour or so to make sure they were okay. Better annoyed than dead.

Gramma Beth was expecting them for dinner in a few minutes, but Noah was out of clean clothes. That was his excuse anyway. She knew what he really wanted was to scan their house to see if Erik had been there while they were away. With little more than a few grumbles, Noah took off to his task before she even had a chance to shut off the engine.

Winter watched him go, a little black-and-yellow device

clenched in his good hand, his gaze fixed to the screen. For weeks now—or even longer—she knew he'd been feeling uncharacteristically powerless about everything happening around them.

He wanted to protect her and their family so desperately that every time something went wrong, he internalized it as some kind of moral failing on his part. And Winter suspected he felt that same way about his own abduction and losing a finger—like it was some kind of burden he'd placed on her because he'd lost a fistfight to a damn car.

And then Erik trying to steal his identity and his cards getting frozen…well, that was the straw that did it. Noah felt guilty. He felt like he was consistently failing at every challenge he faced. Now he was starting to act like he needed to prove himself.

There was nothing he could do—and nothing that could ever happen—that would change Winter's mind about her husband. Not only did she love him, she viewed him with the same amount of respect she always had. The utmost. She wished she could think of a way to make him see that. He sure wasn't listening to her words.

Sighing, Winter stepped out of the SUV and stretched her arms. Her whole body ached from being in the same position for so long. She swung her legs and arms side to side, loosening her tight hips, unashamed to do a little wiggle dance in her driveway to get her body responding again.

For hours now, Winter had been replaying the conversation with Justin in her head, though not the way she usually would. She was proud of her brain and her heart for so easily glossing over her brother's attempts to bait her or make her feel bad. Instead, the only things she cared to think about were the bits of information he'd dropped about Erik Waller.

Erik had clearly had an anxious childhood. On top of

Mom dying, the impression she got was that his father largely ignored him or even disliked him. Erik had spent most of his time alone, playing video games and consuming other media. He had no real friends and had never had a girlfriend, according to Sutherland.

This loneliness and lack of acceptance—combined with his anger and sense of inherent superiority—created a man who thought he had nothing to lose and everything to gain from a world that owed him.

Winter wasn't a psychologist, of course, not like her best friend, Autumn Trent. But she'd spent her life trying to understand deranged personalities. She considered herself fairly skilled at analyzing the motivations of humans who made very little empirical sense. People with no empathy or sense of shame. People who genuinely enjoyed violence and the suffering of others. Broken people with dead eyes and a twisted sense of reality that revolved only around them.

Erik Waller was no different.

In his view, nobody in the world was an actual person except him. He felt so othered, it made it impossible to relate to…anyone. Yet an intense urge to connect clawed at his insides. And because he was narcissistic, perhaps not pathologically but at the very least colloquially, he wanted to connect himself to people he admired and considered successful. People who had done things he'd only ever dreamed about.

This line of thinking led him to his hero worship of Justin. Erik looked at him and saw a man without fear. In Justin, he found a mentor.

Erik clearly didn't understand how vulnerable he'd made himself when he told Justin he wanted to be a part of his family. He didn't understand that Justin became his enemy the second he confessed his attraction to his sister and his desire to marry her.

Winter wrinkled her nose and swallowed hard to keep down the icky taste that always came up when she thought about what Erik really wanted from her.

Justin had humored him at first. Granted, he was likely hard up for entertainment. And he always claimed to love his fans, but only because they made him feel important. Their adoration fed his godlike ego. Like Erik, he loved to explore the lengths to which he could manipulate others, especially if that meant getting them to betray their morals.

Justin quickly grew tired of people who didn't have any morals, though. Nothing to break. Nothing to destroy. In fact, he hated people who were just like him. Probably because, deep down, he hated himself.

She suspected the same was true of Erik Waller.

Justin had likely toyed with him for a little while—seeing what kind of atrocities he could get him to commit. But Erik was too dedicated, too brutal, too much like Justin to actually hold his interest for long.

This rejection hurt Erik. And because the man was emotionally stunted, he mistook the pain of Justin's rejection for anger. Now Erik wanted to prove her brother wrong, wanted to show him up.

Another giant ego out in the world, created to hide scars that would never heal.

The front door opened, and Noah stepped out onto the porch. "Are you coming in?"

Cracking her neck, Winter gave a tired yawn and started up the steps. "Anything?"

"Place seems clean." Noah shrugged and lowered his scanner. "That doesn't mean Erik hasn't been here."

"It's safe to assume he's been everywhere." Winter slumped into a blue Adirondack chair, sitting comfortably beside a large pot of ornamental grass and geraniums.

"Are you okay, darlin'?" Noah set down the detector and

took a seat at her side. "You haven't said much about your talk with Justin."

"I don't want to give him any more attention than is strictly necessary. Honestly, I don't feel a damn thing."

Noah nodded and set his hand on her knee. It was clear he didn't believe her.

"I'm fine." She was quick to catch his fingers in hers and squeeze. "I'm just thinking about what to do next."

"Any ideas?"

Winter bit her lip and looked away. She'd been asking herself the same question for hours. "We should be heading back to my grandparents' house."

Noah nodded, slapping his knees as he stood. "Okay. I just need to get a few things. You need anything?"

She shook her head, staring off at the street as Noah went back into the house. Somewhere in the distance, a dog barked out a halting rhythm. Lavendar skies brooded above, bright and lovely, but they were teeming with silver clouds that churned with threats of rain.

With another sigh that felt like it started all the way down at the bottom of her feet, Winter pushed herself up from the chair. Her boots clomped on the porch as she walked toward the front door and pulled a thick pile of mail from the little bronze box fixed to the siding.

A spring catalog from a local farming store, bills, a book of coupons. Winter made her way toward the big blue recycling bin in the drive. Tomorrow was trash pickup day. There wasn't much in the cans, but she might as well take them out anyway.

Still sorting the mail as she walked, Winter found Noah's stipend check from the FBI and shoved it under her arm. She dropped junk mail in the bin, one envelope at a time, before pausing on a postcard. The photo was of a picturesque forest, sunbeams pouring through cracks in the canopy to illuminate a narrow footpath below.

Her heart lifted, hoping that it might be from Kline—her long-lost biological father who'd blown into her life like a tornado and then disappeared without so much as a goodbye.

"Stop it," she chastised herself. Why did it always take so much time and effort to convince herself to stop caring about people who didn't care about her?

When she flipped over the card, her chest sank. There was no stamp, no return address. Another hand-delivered missive. The blank space on the back was filled with a crude pencil drawing of a house—just a square with a triangle for the roof and something written underneath it.

Finally found our forever home, Hummingbird!

Inside the square portion of the little house was the number 91 and some chicken scratch. She squinted and held the postcard to the light.

"'Tiny, deadly, silky,'" she read aloud.

Winter's lip twitched. She glanced at the triangle, reread the main message, and reread the riddle.

"The fu—"

The screen door slapped the frame as it swung shut, and she startled as Noah stepped onto the porch, a duffel bag slung over his shoulder. With his left hand in the pocket of his loose sweatpants, Noah stalked closer. Winter looked into his dark-green eyes and held the card out to him.

He snatched it up and turned it over in his hands, the wrinkles between his brows deepening. "Erik fucking Waller." His lips narrowed in anger. "What does it mean?"

"He's obsessed with the idea of starting a family with…" Winter cut off the end of the sentence.

"With what?"

She looked down, knowing how much it would upset her

husband. Knowing he didn't have much room left in his brain for more anger and frustration. Still, the last thing she needed was to hold information back from him and try to handle things on her own. She'd promised herself when they got married that she wouldn't do that anymore.

"With me."

Noah's eyes flashed. His fingers squeaked where they gripped the postcard too tight.

"I think he found 'our' new home. He's getting everything ready. Someday soon, he's going to pop the question."

"Pop the question?" Noah laughed so loud that it almost sounded like a scream. "You're already married."

"Why do you think he had Lessner cut off your ring finger?" Winter cringed at her own words when the shadow fell over her husband's face. "Erik's orders. He wants you dead. He's not done trying."

Dread wove a path under her skin as she envisioned Justin leaning over her—telling her that they were going to be together forever. Licking his lips and promising that the day was coming when he'd take everything from her.

Justin had planned on making her his wife, too, in a way. Erik Waller was no different. If he got her alone and incapacitated, there was no telling the horrors he'd subject her to. A fate worse than death was what he had planned. Every day Erik remained free, he crept closer to that goal.

"I won't let that happen." Noah's rough hand touched her face gently.

She examined his face, heart clenching at the mask of determination it held. But she knew him too well. She could see the fear he was hiding.

Erik had kidnapped Noah already, and if not for his obsessive game-playing, Noah would already be dead. Why should Winter or anyone else be any different?

"C'mon, babe." Winter threaded her fingers through his and started back to the SUV. "Let's go."

20

After having dinner with her grandparents, Winter sat in the corner of the sofa in their living room and stared at the soft flames in the gas-powered fireplace. She drew her knees up against her chest, arms wrapped around them, with Erik's postcard balanced on the armrest beside her. She felt dirty from being on a plane with recirculated air and a little bit sick, but she hadn't been able to convince herself to get up and take a shower.

Normal tasks all seemed so unimportant compared to the frantic whirl of ugly thoughts in her brain. A serial killer was trying to murder everyone she loved and turn her into his slave. Also, she needed to run a load of laundry. How the hell was anybody supposed to manage such wildly different priorities?

Jaya Bakshi and her quiet tears dripped gently in the back of Winter's brain. She couldn't stop thinking about her and her family—how they fit into Erik's grand scheme and what sort of plans he might have for them. She'd spoken to Darnell last night. There'd been no news on Manoj Bakshi. But when she'd called on the way over, his phone had gone to voicemail.

He'd call back soon. She knew him well enough to trust in that. Still, she felt unreasonably angry that he wasn't at her beck and call. What else could he possibly be doing?

Maybe his laundry had piled up too.

The most nagging question at the moment was—how was Manoj Bakshi involved in Erik's plans? Winter's fingers played absently over the furry blanket covering her knees. Perhaps if she talked to other members of his family or his coworkers, she'd be able to reveal some kind of weakness or even a hobby that had drawn Erik to him. Moms didn't always know what their teens were up to.

Erik needed a new lackey. A new Harlan Lessner or Cybil Kerie to do his dirty work. Both of them had been tragic individuals with a desire for revenge. Perhaps Manoj Bakshi shared those characteristics.

She took out her phone to make sure the ringer and notifications were on. They were. She checked the time. Almost nine. There was a decent chance Darnell wouldn't get back to her until tomorrow morning.

Her stubby fingernails twitched over the postcard, which she'd read again and again. Erik was trying to guide her toward a specific location—a party she would be remiss not to attend. She'd taken a picture of the image on front and tried to search the location from that, but the internet returned nothing.

"A square with the number ninety-one and..." She chewed softly on her bottom lip. "Tiny, deadly, silky..."

"A spider?"

Winter looked up as Gramma Beth ambled into the room. "What?"

"Tiny, deadly, silky. The answer is a spider."

Winter's lips parted. She looked down at the card, then back at Gramma. "Why didn't I think of that?"

"Stress is not good for thinking." Gramma Beth wore a silk bonnet over her hair and a thin cotton robe over her purple nightgown. She didn't appear to allow stress an inch. "Can I get you anything more, dearie? Another serving of cobbler?"

"Thanks, Gramma, but I'm stuffed." She forced a smile, even as her fingertips brushed the postcard.

Gramma Beth padded closer on fuzzy slippers and sat down in her favorite puffy chair across from where Winter was curled up on the sofa.

"Okay, so it's a spider." She handed the postcard to her grandmother. "What's the rest of this mean?"

The older woman lifted her brows and squinted at the card, holding it far away from her face. Setting it down, she riffled through a small box on the table beside her and took out her reading glasses.

Winter drummed her fingers on the sofa cushion. "I think it's a location. He sent his message in code last time."

Gramma Beth nodded sharply and handed back the card. "The answer is eight."

Winter waited for her brain to catch up. She was more tired than she'd realized. "What?"

"A spider has eight legs. And that sketch is a house."

"Eight. Duh." Winter conked herself on the forehead. "What's wrong with me tonight?"

"Nothing. I just do a lot of crosswords." Gramma Beth grinned proudly.

"Eight." Winter massaged her temples, silently begging her brain to work. "Ninety-one and eight. Nine, one, eight… a house number?"

"Most likely. So I guess you'll be sleeping here again?"

Winter nodded. "Mm-hmm. Of course."

"You don't have to, you know. I mean, you're always welcome, but you gotta be gettin' tired of hanging out with the old people all the time."

Winter slapped her hand over the postcard and stared hard at her grandmother. "I just want to make sure you're safe."

"I know that, dearie. But I also know you've got bigger fish to fry." Gramma Beth smoothed the fabric of her gown over her lap. "There's something I've been meaning to tell you. Your grampa said we ought to wait 'til everything's settled, but with all your worries over us, I think you deserve to know."

A fresh wave of anxiety curdled in her stomach. "What's up?"

"There ain't no easy way to say this, so I'm just gonna say it. Winter honey, your grampa and I have decided to sell the house."

Winter's jaw dropped. "Which house?"

"This house, silly."

"You can't do that."

"Your grampa's lupus needs close monitoring, and I'm worried about what might happen if my kidneys get worse. It's about time we got ourselves into a place that's all on one floor. Those stairs are gonna be the death of us both." She chuckled lightly under her breath, but it was a wholly sad sound.

Words failed Winter. She tried to say something, but only a squeak came out.

Gramma Beth flattened an imaginary wrinkle in her gown. "We're no spring chickens. Our doctor recommended an independent senior living facility right here in Austin. They also have an assisted living option. And what with everything that's been happening with you lately…we've decided it's time."

"I don't…" Winter blinked slowly. "Is that seriously what you want?"

Gramma Beth sighed and glanced around her living room with a wistful grin. "We love this house. But it just isn't practical for us anymore. Your grampa needs more care than I can give him."

"I can help out. We could hire a nurse."

"Baby girl." Gramma Beth reached across the space between them and set her hand on Winter's knees. "It's high time you start focusing on your own family. You and your husband, maybe a few little ones someday."

"Little what?" What was her grandmother talking about? "Cats?"

"I know you must be tired. You're goofy."

"Me? You're the one talking crazy."

Her mouth tugged sideways in that way that always meant she was about to say something you wouldn't like. "You're not getting any younger, either, you know."

Three people now calling her old. What the hell was going on?

Winter bit her bottom lip. "We could move everything down from the attic. Put your bedroom in the den. Then you wouldn't have to worry about the stairs."

"And what about Ada Smith, hmm?"

"Who?"

"Ada Smith who, until recently, lived just down the street? She's two years younger than me. Slipped and fell while trying to step over the tub to get out of the shower. Broke her arm and her hip. Stayed helpless on her bathroom floor for a day and a half before her grandson came by and found her. I don't ever want that to happen to me."

"It never would. You don't live alone. Even then, I'd come find you."

"I want you not to have to worry about me. That's the

whole point." Gramma Beth laughed and shook her head. "The place we've been looking at…we'd still have our own little apartment. We'll have meals prepared for us but have our own kitchen, so you can still come for Sunday dinners. We'll have a nice balcony overlooking a river, and elevators to get up and down the floors. We'll have nurses to help us. And we'll have a whole community to spend our time with."

"Huh." Winter grasped for some argument that would make her case, but she had to admit Gramma Beth was making some good points.

"I've thought about it a lot. I'll miss our house, but we need to do what's right for us now."

Winter nodded, her gaze dropping. Her grandparents had clearly made up their minds. There was no point arguing. "If that's what you want…"

"It is, dearie. It really is."

"Okay." Her voice came out small and crackly. *Can Noah and I come with you?* It took everything inside Winter not to ask.

"It won't be for another few weeks at least. We're on a waiting list." Gramma Beth's knees popped as she stood. She kissed the top of Winter's head. "I love you, honey."

"I love you too, Gramma."

"I'm heading to bed. You should do the same soon."

"Another few minutes and I will."

Winter watched as her grandmother made her way up the switchback stairs toward the second floor. She'd never noticed until this moment just how slowly Gramma Beth ascended the stairs—hand gripping the rail, bringing both feet onto one step before moving to the next.

The last thing Winter wanted to think about was her grandparents getting older. Her heart simply couldn't even consider another loss.

Don't think about it now.

When her grandmother disappeared from view, Winter opened her phone. She thought about calling Eve, but it was almost ten.

She badly wanted to call her, but the hour was more appropriate for bugging a young, childless woman, so Winter scrolled to her assistant's name and tapped Call. She'd tasked Ariel with finding out more about the Bakshi family—the mom, the grandfather, and Manoj's little brother, Hari. She was especially curious about the circumstances surrounding the death of Mr. Bakshi, wondering if his death might have something to do with Erik's interest in the teen.

"Hello?" Ariel answered after several rings. She sounded tired, like perhaps Winter had woken her.

Oops.

"Hey, Ariel. Is this a bad time? Please tell me if it is."

"No. Now's perfect."

Winter didn't believe her completely but didn't argue. "Do you have anything new to tell me?"

Ariel yawned again, though it sounded faded this time, like she'd pulled the phone away from her mouth. "Yeah. I looked into Manoj's dad, Arjun Bakshi. He immigrated to the U.S. from India when he was sixteen. No criminal record, no debt. Nothing really. He worked most of his life in construction. I called his old company and talked to one of his coworkers. The guy didn't have a single bad thing to say about him."

"How'd he die?"

"An accident on-site. Someone didn't secure a beam properly. It slipped loose and fell on him. He was in a coma for a few weeks and then passed away."

Life was so unfair to so many.

"Did Jaya sue? Was she compensated?"

"I was still looking into that. I think she got a small settlement, enough to pay for the funeral and medical bills. I don't think she got much else, since she had to pack up her kids and move to a new city to stay with her father."

Winter shifted on the sofa. "How long ago?"

"Almost ten years. His youngest son was only a few months old." Ariel gave another long yawn. "I'll have more for you tomorrow morning."

"Okay. Go get some sleep. See you in the morning."

"You too." Ariel hung up.

Winter found herself twitching in her seat. She checked her email and did her own online search on the name Arjun Bakshi to no avail. Eventually, she realized she was wasting her time, so she peeled herself off the sofa and headed out to the back porch where her husband and grandfather were sitting on the swing and talking, cold beers in hand.

Hearing their laughter, Winter paused at the screen and rested her forehead on the frame. Their happiness made her heart swell in the most pleasant way.

"My advice to you, son," Grampa Jack said, "you just need to *get a grip*."

Winter's jaw dropped.

"Thanks, Gramps," Noah's voice was flat. "You're the bee's knees."

"Touché." Grampa Jack winked, and Noah responded with a genuine laugh.

Winter had an urge to shout at both of them for being so callous, but hearing Noah laugh, she couldn't help smiling. Even if it was all in terrible taste. What did she expect, marrying a Marine?

She decided to let them have their weird fun and drifted off toward the bedroom, shaking her head as she went.

21

Hari Bakshi woke with a start, gasped for air, and immediately panicked. The memory of what he'd just experienced flashed through his mind like a nightmare on a loop. His dada's blood sprinkled his skin like acid as he fell with a thud, blood pooling from the hole in his head. Hari crying, pleading, screaming unintelligible gibberish.

He thrashed, needing to run away from both the memories and this place, but could barely move. His arms and legs were held fast in place by scratchy ties. At last, he peeled open his eyes, but he struggled to focus in the darkness.

Despite choking on his own saliva and tears, Hari tried to scream. What came out was a pathetic wheeze, like an animal in the final throes of panic before submitting to a tranquilizer.

Hari clenched his eyes shut again, telling himself to wake up. He told himself none of this could really be real. Any moment now, his maata would lay her hand on his cheek and tell him to wake up and get ready for school. He'd breathe in and smell roti and dal cooking. Any moment now, his cat would jump on his face and start kneading his neck like bread. Any moment now…

Tears stung his eyes as he opened them again. This time, after blinking rapidly, he was able to make out shapes and faint color in the dark room. He looked down at his body and inspected the twine wrapped around his hands, holding him fast to a wooden dining chair. Black dots stained his jeans and orange t-shirt.

Across the room, high up near the ceiling, some kind of artificial light poured through cracks of a little rectangular window that seemed to be held together with duct tape.

Wheezing echoed all around him. Assuming he was alone, Hari pressed his teeth together and exhaled through his nose to quiet his breathing. The noise didn't stop.

He scanned the room until his gaze landed on another chair tucked in a far corner. A man was tied to it. He blinked repeatedly again, his eyes and mind adjusting to the environment. He stared at the man's white Converse sneakers and red laces. It took some time before the truth slammed into him like a bullet train. The dark, curly hair, the clothes…

Manoj?

He wanted to say his name out loud but was afraid to make any noise. Glancing around to make sure no one was watching, Hari wiggled and pulled against the ties.

Manoj wheezed again and again, and Hari realized he was having an asthma attack. His brother had suffered from the condition as long as he could remember. When they'd be out playing basketball or even just riding their bikes, Manoj would often have to stop and take a pull of his inhaler. Their maata never ceased to nag him about making sure he had it with him.

Fortunately, Manoj didn't suffer from attacks too often,

but when they did happen, they had the power to bring him to his knees or worse.

Manoj needed his inhaler.

The twine scratched and tore at the back of Hari's hand, but he managed to twist his wrist around so his palm faced up. He found the knot with the very tips of his fingers and began to pull at the fibers. His brother needed his help. He had to dig his inhaler from his pocket, assuming it was still there, and they had to get out before the man with the gun came back.

As if summoned by his fear, just as one of the knots tying his wrists together loosened, the door at the top of the basement stairs opened with a bang. Though Hari knew he had enough wiggle room now to pull his hand free, he stayed frozen in place.

The stairs creaked as the man moved closer, one slow, heavy step at a time. He had an electric camping lantern in his hand, illuminating the basement more with each step.

At last, Hari got a clear view of his brother's face. Manoj's eyes were wide open, staring right back at him. He was covered in bruises and tiny tears, his complexion sickly green. He'd been gagged by what seemed like a plastic-coated charging cable—wrapped around and around his head, inside his mouth. It pulled back the corners of his lips like a horse with a bit.

Hari's chest heaved, more tears threatening. He began to shake as the man stepped into view. His hair was wet and slicked back like he'd just had a shower, his clothes clean. His yellow t-shirt declared *I play the keyboard* across the front in old-school computer font.

Walking toward Manoj, the man placed the lantern near his feet and set both hands on his knees as he hunched down to gaze at his face. Manoj pulled back hard, hissing behind his cable gag. His breathing grew even more pained. With a laugh, the man very slowly turned his face over one shoulder to stare at Hari.

The man who killed his dada had empty eyes. No light. No emotion. They were just dead. He wasn't a man at all. Not even an animal. Hari didn't know what he was, but there was no way he was human.

"It's a good thing you're here." The man straightened and took a few steps toward Hari. The lantern glowed behind him, casting a long black shadow. He reached into his jeans pocket and took out an inhaler.

Hari stared at the device before glancing at his brother. His breath was growing shallower now. Weaker and weaker with each passing moment.

"Do you know what happened to people with asthma before inhalers were invented?"

Hari hardened his gaze, letting his hatred shine through his eyes as he stared daggers at the man. Yet he couldn't help looking back at his brother as the strength left his chest.

"That's right. They choked to death on their own broken lungs. Do you think that's what's going on here?"

Hari screamed behind his gag. He looked down, knowing he could get his hand free. But then what?

"I'm Erik, by the way. And you're Harry, isn't that right?" The man—Erik—smiled and tossed the inhaler at Hari's feet. "Let's play another game, hmm? I'm finna give you one chance to save him. Just like your gramps. Let's hope your luck is better this time, yeah?"

Hari looked at the inhaler and then back at Erik. He wanted to tell him he wasn't going to play his stupid games anymore. The man walked back over to Manoj and stood at the side of his chair. He smiled like a wolf baring his teeth and kicked the chair onto its side. Manoj crashed to the ground with a pain-filled grunt. His head struck the concrete, and his wheezing increased. He began to twitch and spasm, his eyes rolling into the back of his head.

"Hurry up, Harry. You'd better get him his medicine. I don't think he has much longer."

As the man retreated and took a seat on the bottom step, Hari yanked his one hand free of the ties. Erik audibly gasped as Hari tore at the twine on his other wrist with his fingernails. Once both his hands were free, he bent over and untied the knots holding his legs to the chair. Standing, he scooped up the inhaler and stumbled to where his brother lay, his breath so shallow and his eyes sinking.

Hari fumbled with the knotted wire. His fingers were numb and thick, like they had no feeling. He'd stood up so fast, all the blood had rushed to his head, and his limbs tingled from being stuck in one spot for so long. He couldn't get the knot undone, so he pulled it tighter to get some slack in the wire and yanked it down over his brother's bottom lip. One loop at a time, gaining more slack with each freed coil.

At last, Hari got the last twist of wire out of his brother's mouth so all of it hung loose around his neck. Blood trickled from the corners of Manoj's lips.

Hari shook the inhaler like he'd seen his brother do, stuck the device in his mouth, and depressed the dispenser, which made that characteristic cough as medicine flowed. Nothing happened. Manoj's head lay limp against the concrete, his eyes half closed.

Was he too late?

"No, no, no, no." He smacked his brother's cheek and shook the device before shoving it in his mouth and depressing the canister again. "No! You can't! Manoj, please. Inhale when I release the medicine, please!"

Every bone trembled as horror closed in all around Hari. He was too late. Just like with his grandfather, he'd been given a chance to save him and failed. His brother was dead, and it was his fault.

Hari started to cry when Manoj's lips tightened around the mouthpiece. Hari pressed the dispenser again and again, and each of Manoj's breaths became slower, deeper, and more controlled.

"Manoj?" Hari cleared the snot and tears from his face with the back of his hand. "It's okay. You're okay. You're alive."

"Thank you." Manoj coughed again, bringing pink slime to his lips. "Hari. Are you okay?"

His mouth hung open at his brother's question. There was no answer.

Crouching in front of his brother like an angry cat, Hari cast a furious glance to where Erik sat on the stairs, his pistol trained on them.

"He's alive." Hari clenched his teeth so hard his jaw ached. "You lose."

Erik chuckled and shook his head. "That's not the game. You know the game."

Only then did Hari notice the three playing cards lying face down on the floor at Erik's feet. His heart turned to ice in his chest, the droplets of his grandfather's acidic blood flaring back to life.

"No."

"Find the lady, Harry."

"No."

Erik scratched his temple with the barrel of his gun, his smile growing.

Who points a loaded gun at their own head? This guy is as whacked as they come.

"Find the lady, and your brother can go free. You've already proven you're the one I really want, not him."

His words were like a sharp icicle stabbing through his lungs. "Me? Why?"

"You'll see. But first, we've got to get rid of this one. He's useless. I don't really care either way, but since you belong to me now, I figured, why not give you a chance? That's all life is, don't you know that, Harry? It's a game of chance."

"He's lying." Manoj gasped and spat on the ground in contempt. "Stay away from my brother, you sick fuck!"

"If you won't play, he's dead anyway. Why not give it a shot?" Erik laughed, tossing his head back. Tiny droplets of water from his wet hair sprinkled the air. "Give it a shot. Do you get it?"

"Don't listen to him, Hari. He's just screwing with you. I swear, if you touch my brother, I'll—"

"You'll what, Señor Tied to a Chair? You're bleeding from your eyes. What you finna do, bro?"

With a final glance at his fuming brother, Hari rose to his feet and stumbled closer to Erik and his cards. "Please. Don't hurt him. I don't know what you want, but I'll do anything. Just, please—"

"He's lying!" Manoj screamed. "Don't do anything this shit stain wants!"

"See why I don't want you no more?" Erik's smile hardened into a sneer as he glared at Manoj. Then his eyes flicked to Hari. "Find the lady, Harry. She's the only one who can help you."

Hari closed his eyes hard to keep himself from looking back at his brother. Before he could second-guess his decision, he crouched in front of the cards and stared at them. He'd picked wrong last time. He couldn't make the same mistake again.

"Om Gam Ganapataye Namah." Hari spoke under his breath and closed his eyes tight, praying the universe would lead his hand to the right choice. To get through this, he

needed to see without his eyes and feel without his hands. He called out silently to the spirit of his dada for forgiveness and help. He called out to his maata, wherever she was, hoping she could feel him and that her love would guide his hand.

None of the cards called to him, though. None seemed safer than any other. None glowed in his mind's eye with a light of redemption. Gazing out through his physical eyes, each looked as black as all the others.

"Ticktock, Harry." Erik tilted his head from side to side. "I'll give you five more seconds. Five, four, three, two—"

Hari snatched the card in the middle and flipped it.

Suicide jack.

"Whomp whomp." Erik's dead eyes sparkled as he raised the gun.

"Wait!"

But just like the first time, the shot went off. The blast was so close that Hari's hearing went blank.

Silence wrapped about his head.

A high-pitched ringing busted through the barrier, along with the hideous sounds of choking. With both hands tangled in his black curls and pulling hard, Hari looked back at his brother. Blood bloomed on his chest. His head lay slumped on the concrete, eyes hooding over. Blood flowed from his body like a creeping river and encircled the inhaler.

Hari scrambled to his brother, the knees of his pants soaking up blood. "Manoj!" He snatched up the inhaler and held it to his brother's mouth. "You can't. You have to hold on. Please."

Manoj lifted his hand and laid it over Hari's fingers. Their eyes met. Manoj tried to speak but choked on his words and shut his eyes completely.

"No." Hari shoved the inhaler in his brother's mouth and pushed the depressor. "No! You can't! Please!"

"Brah. He's dead."

"No, no, no." Hari clenched his eyes shut. Manoj couldn't be dead. This couldn't be happening. It was just a nightmare. It had to be a nightmare.

Hari began to cough, which led into dry-heaving. He grasped his belly as yellow slime slid down his chin. It wasn't real. It couldn't be real. He was having a nightmare and all he had to do was wake up. "Maata…" He hugged his shoulders so tight that it hurt. "Please."

"You really suck at this game." Erik laughed deep in his throat. "Sucks to be your family, huh?"

Rage rushed through Hari like the crack of a whip. His sight went red. He leaped to his feet and rushed at Erik, ready to die along with his brother if it meant getting his claws in his killer first. "You're dead!"

Erik snarled and backhanded him with the hand that held the gun. Hard metal smacked his jaw. Hari screamed in pain and fell back, hitting the concrete with his spine.

"You better watch yourself, fam. Don't think you're irreplaceable."

Lying on the cold concrete, the smell of his brother's blood and death in the air—it smelled horrible now that he thought of it—Hari curled in on himself again. From the corner of his eyes, Hari glimpsed the cards. The suicide jack lay face up between the others.

As Erik gloated over him, Hari inched closer to the cards. He reached out a trembling hand and flipped one—the king of diamonds—and then the other.

The ace of spades.

There was no queen. It didn't matter which one he picked. It had never mattered.

Growling, the man stomped closer. "Get away from there."

"There is no lady…"

"I said get away!" Erik grabbed Hari by his arm and

yanked him up to his knees. Hari didn't look away from the cards. Suicide jack, king of diamonds, ace of spades…

"You were going to kill him no matter what. You cheated!"

"Life is rigged, Harry. That's your first lesson." Erik crouched in front of Hari and pulled a long piece of twine from the deep pockets of his baggy jeans. Hari was so numb, so outside of his own body, that he barely felt it as Erik yanked his feet out and tied his ankles together.

It occurred to him to try to fight back. To kick and scream and try to get Erik to kill him too, but it was as if someone had severed Hari's body from his brain. He was screaming inside, but his lips were silent. He was thrashing inside, but his body was as limp as a fresh corpse.

As a corpse. Like his dada. Like Manoj.

It couldn't be true. It wasn't real. It couldn't be real. It just couldn't be.

"Maata…" He could barely understand his own voice through numb lips.

Erik snatched his arms and fastened his wrists together so tightly, it felt like they'd start bleeding. Hari didn't struggle. He blinked and looked back at his brother's blood shining like an oil slick on the floor.

Wake up. He closed his eyes tight enough to sting. *Please wake up.*

But he would never wake up. The nightmare was real. And there was no escape.

22

When Winter arrived at her office at eight the next morning, a person was sitting on the concrete just outside with their back against the glass doors. They had their knees tucked up near their chest and wore a long yellow shawl and cowl. Fear jolted through Winter, and she stopped so abruptly that her mocha latte spilled through the tiny hole in its plastic lid. Her mind immediately flashed to Erik, as it so often did these days.

The slight figure suggested a woman, and the shawl was distinctly feminine, but Winter didn't trust such things. Justin had never been shy about gender-bending, and Erik Waller seemed cut from a similar cloth. It was only when she caught sight of a delicate hand with deep-brown skin that Winter breathed out a heavy sigh and continued her approach.

She paused when she was about three yards away. "Excuse me?"

The person turned, and Winter was taken aback by the pain on her face. Red puffiness encircled her big eyes, and long wrinkles were deep around her lips and between her brows.

"Jaya?"

Jaya Bakshi held her skirt and her shawl as she scrambled to her feet. Tears trembled in her eyes, and she reached out her small hands. "Please. I need your help, Mrs. Black."

"What happened?" Winter closed the space between them. "Are you all right?"

"My father is dead. My son…my Hari. That man took him. Please. I need someone to help me. Please! I have nowhere else to go."

As she pulled the woman into her arms, Winter's words of sympathy were cut off by her ringing phone. She knew who it was before she even dug it out of her purse. She apologized to Jaya before answering, "Darnell?"

"Black. Bad news—"

"Manoj Bakshi's grandfather is dead, and his little brother Hari is missing."

"How'd you—"

"Jaya is sitting outside my office door. Distraught."

"Well, don't go taking this investigation into your own hands. I know how you roll. Call me as soon as you can."

"Will do, Darnell." Winter hung up and motioned for Jaya to follow her.

Jaya had clearly been teetering at the edge of hysterics for a while now. Winter suffered a visceral pain of empathy, seeing herself from only a week prior in Jaya's thick tears.

"Come on. Come inside and tell me what happened." She inched past Jaya, and her keys jingled as she opened the door. Stepping inside, she flicked on the light and set down her satchel and coffee cup on Ariel's desk.

"Someone broke into my house while I was working. They shot my father. He was sitting at the kitchen table doing a jigsaw puzzle. They shot him. The same man who kidnapped Manoj shot him." Jaya's hand went to her mouth.

Winter tried to speak but was hit with a heavy lump in her throat.

Jaya closed her eyes for a slow breath. "Why would anyone do this to my family? We have never hurt anyone. Everyone in the community loved my father. And my *jaanu*, my Hari. The man took him. I know he did! He was home, decorating the house to cheer me up. He was in the middle of it. I can't…why is this happening to us?"

Winter accidentally made a horrible noise that sounded like a precursor to her own tears. The urge to fight or flee gnawed at the back of her neck. She didn't want to tell Jaya what she believed had transpired. She didn't want to tell her any more about what she suspected might've happened to her two sons or the character of the man she believed shot her father.

"The police have been there, correct?" She knew they had but had to ask, had to hear Jaya's story.

Jaya nodded, looking down at the floor. "Yes. I came home late, past eleven, and walked into my kitchen, and I saw…" She shook her head.

When Jaya began to tremble again, Winter laid a gentle hand on the woman's slight shoulder. "I'm going to help you. Take a deep breath. Come. Sit with me."

Jaya moved like a dry leaf in the wind as Winter led her to the couch near the back of the office, and they sat down together. Jaya took a handkerchief secured to one wrist with a rubber band and wiped her eyes.

"I called the police. They came and roped off my house. They can't tell me who did it. They haven't found Manoj. My Hari is missing. They could see his footprints in…in…"

Winter didn't want to imagine the scene, but when she

blinked, all she saw was blood. She waited for Jaya to control her emotions to finish her sentence.

"They found two sets of shoe prints in my father's blood. Hari's size, his sneakers, and another's, much bigger."

"Where were you when this happened?"

Jaya sat up straight with her hands poised on her knees, but she didn't answer right away. She closed her eyes for a moment, composing herself. "I had shown several houses yesterday in rural areas. I did so much driving. But then my clients wanted to put in an offer, so I was at the office very late. Writing it up."

Winter nodded slowly, the wheels in her mind turning. "You're in real estate."

"Yes. I work for a small firm."

"What area of the city?"

"Why does it matter?"

Winter pressed her lips together. "Some of my questions may not seem important, but I need you to just give me as much information as you can."

Clearly, Jaya was irritated, and who could blame her? "Okay. I specialize in more rural property these days. I grew up on a small farm, so I have better luck than many working with those kinds of customers."

Winter rose to her feet to pace the carpet. If Erik Waller was behind all the tragedy that had befallen the Bakshi family, then he'd likely been watching them for a long time. Erik didn't do anything without sitting back to observe first. They knew he'd spent time inside Black Cherry market.

Something in his ego made Erik want to be directly involved in his victim's lives in one way or another, often before he perpetrated any evil against them. She thought of Noah's run-in with the man at the park just a few days before he'd ordered Lessner to kidnap him.

If the pattern held, she'd bet anything Jaya had already met the man too.

It was worth a shot. Winter went to her briefcase, pulled out her laptop, and carried it back to the couch. She sat and opened the laptop on her knees, her fingers tapping in quick succession against her leg as it booted up. She went into her ever-growing file on Erik Saulson—no, Waller—and pulled up the photo from his college days.

"Do you recognize this man?"

Jaya's brow furrowed as she leaned in closer to the screen. "I know him."

Winter's stomach twisted into a tight knot. "When?"

"Maybe two months ago. I'm not sure. He called me up and asked to see a specific place I had listed."

"Did he tell you his name?"

"Walter Erikson."

Winter scoffed deep in her throat. How very creative. "Did he purchase the house?"

She nodded. "I represented him in the sale. I was very happy to get a commission on a cabin that had been on the market a while. Cute enough, but isolated. The sale was quick. I didn't spend any time with him besides the initial showing and the closing."

"Can you give me the address?"

"You think this is the man who did this to my family?" Jaya rose to her feet, her small hands clenching into fists as hard as stones. "I will take you to the cabin."

"I don't think that's such a good idea."

"This man killed my father. He took my babies. I will not sit by while anyone else handles him."

Winter bit the corner of her lip. It was a terrible idea. At the same time, she had to admire Jaya's tenacity. And she knew for a fact that if their places were reversed, she'd never let herself be left behind. Her own feet were already itching to run out the door and race to the address—guns drawn and banners flying.

She took a deep breath. "Walter Erikson's real name is Erik Waller, and he's a very dangerous person. I don't know what we might find at his cabin. And I can't guarantee your safety."

"Nobody can." Jaya set her jaw hard, her tears once again a memory as fury shrank her pupils into pinpricks. "I will take you there. I will not tell you where it is."

"Dammit." Winter pinched the bridge of her nose. It was clear neither of them had the patience for this argument. "Fine. But I'm driving. And you have to promise to tell me the address on the way, so I can contact the police and have them meet us there. Unless we both want to end up his victims, we can't do this alone."

Jaya's lips grew thin and long across her face, and her eyes flicked toward the window. Winter looked too. Outside, a beautiful spring day was blooming—white blossoms shivering on the trees. It felt backward, almost as if the sun were laughing at them, since the atmosphere inside the tiny office was better suited to a stormy night.

"I will do as you say." Jaya nodded sharply and stepped past Winter toward the door. "Let's go."

23

Hari wriggled in my arms. I released him, and he hit the inside of the trunk with a hard thud. I liked the noise he made, so I smiled before slamming the lid and resting my back against the bumper.

My back ached in protest, and the throbbing pain in my thigh was keeping me grounded, that was for sure. And it was getting worse. I'd taken the antibiotics and smeared on all the creams. I washed the wound religiously. To try to combat the pain, I was taking so many pills that my brain was working at half capacity. That was still enough, though. Most people were so stupid, they couldn't keep up with me if I were literally unconscious.

But I had to move, and the kid was coming with me.

I didn't know for sure how long it would take Winter to find the cabin, but I knew she'd find it eventually. And now that I'd had to take a second Bakshi kid and eliminate their gramps, I imagined she was motivated to decode the game even faster. This wasn't the place I'd planned for our first meeting, though, and time was running short. I needed to hurry up and get her surprise ready.

Hari was a fighter, but I'd train him and bring out his darker side. Brainwashing and manipulation to tear apart the boy's will and recircuit his mind didn't necessarily appeal to me. Who had the time? But Hari was young like that kid Justin dealt with, so it should be less of a chore than it would've been with Manoj. I bristled, irked that I had to fall back on Justin's "younger is better" thinking.

I shifted my thoughts to bigger, better, and more beautiful things.

Face-to-face with Winter Black at last. I wanted to giggle every time I thought about it. Our time was drawing so close. It'd take some time with Hari, though. Either I'd get him on board, or I'd get rid of him and find somebody else. It didn't really matter. Though I'd hoped our new son would be ready and at my side when his mother came home.

We'd have children of our own, of course. Someday. But there was so much work to be done before then.

My sneakers slid a little in the dirt as I headed back into the cabin. I had to pause at the porch to ramp up my determination before I dragged my complaining leg up three steps. Heading into the bathroom, I yanked down my pants and sat on the edge of the tub. The gauze over my wound had seeped through with yellow and brown pus, loads of it. I didn't want to look, but I also didn't want it leaking through my jeans.

I gagged on the putrid smell of my own rotting body and wound more bandages around it to keep the outside dry. I couldn't afford to step away from my plans for Winter, as that might give her the chance to catch me with my figurative pants down.

Just a few more days, and she'd be with me. Once I had her under my thumb and in the secure location, I could take the time to kidnap a doctor and force them to fix my leg. 'Til then, I'd tough it out.

"Dammit, Lessner." I ripped the tape with my teeth and secured my new bandage. "I oughta kill you for this a second time."

Pulling up my pants and buckling my belt, I headed into my makeshift bedroom. Only a week ago, I would've been fastidious about cleaning up all trace evidence of myself. Frankly, I didn't give a shit anymore. Let them find out who I really was. Let them find out where I'd been. By the time the cops and those morons in the FBI figured it out, Winter, Hari, and I would be long gone.

I scooped my duffel bag off the floor of my bedroom and went through the house, gathering my things. My car was already stuffed to the brim with what I needed for Winter's surprise, and with Hari in the trunk, there was no room for what little furniture I had. It was all cheap, replaceable shit I bought off the internet under an assumed identity, so I didn't care. And the house I was headed to already had a bed, so I left my air mattress.

I went through the kitchen to collect my food, leaving the garbage for the cops to sift through. I paused to pop three little pink pills and a big blue one—a combination that was quickly becoming my favorite. Turning on the kitchen tap, I used my hand to gather some water and washed them down.

Looking at the stairs leading down into the basement, I felt vaguely threatened. Going down wasn't nearly as bad as coming up, though. And with all my drugs having a party in my gut, I was pretty confident my pain would be all but gone by the time I climbed back up. Dragging Hari up the stairs—the stupid bastard refused to cooperate—had nearly broken me.

Keeping my one leg straight, I navigated the stairs, as the railing was no longer any good to me, also thanks to Lessner.

I paused at the bottom of the steps, dizzy. The pills were kicking in. I had a marker in my back pocket, but that nice little pool of Manoj's blood was a better sort of ink. His inhaler was right next to it. So close. *Too bad, so sad, Manoj.*

Winter had half my riddle already, but she always needed a bit of handholding. With my ungloved fingertip—because who gave a shit at this point—I drew a big square on the concrete with his blood. Then I gathered more blood on my finger and wrote a numeral thirteen inside the square.

Then, outside it—I had to use the marker, as this was taking too long—I wrote my riddle.

1 is 3 and 3 is 5, Apple Blossom!

For a second I hesitated, wondering if I should give her more to run with. Screw it. Either she figured it out, or I didn't actually want her. Last thing I needed was another stupid bitch to deal with.

Winter would work it out. I had every confidence in her. And when she did, she'd come running, like always. And I'd be ready for her.

24

Winter pulled to the side of the road under the canopy of a large oak. The cabin was a good twenty minutes outside Austin's city limits on a lonely dirt road that twisted and wound through heavy forest.

It had been built of whole logs, an actual log cabin getaway. A porch wrapped around the front and one side, with a free-moving swing dangling from the overhang by thick chains. Light fixtures flanking the front door were shaped like lanterns. The building sat on a nice chunk of land that was waking up from the cold weather, the verdant greens of summer beginning to pop up all over.

Winter's heart broke when she thought how such a picturesque place—someone's relaxing retreat at one point—had been converted into Erik's Hideout of Horrors.

Popping open the door, she swung out her legs and pulled the pistol from her ankle holster before stepping out.

En route, Winter had made phone calls to Eve to alert the FBI and to Darnell to alert the APD. She advised Darnell to send an ambulance, too, just in case.

Naturally, given their head start, Winter and Jaya arrived before any of the others.

While Winter wondered how long they should wait and tried to mentally prepare herself for what might happen, Jaya was out of the car and already walking down the path.

Winter jogged after her. "Wait!"

Jaya didn't look back. "My sons might be here. I will wait for nothing."

"You're not going to help your sons by getting yourself killed."

She turned on Winter, venom burning in her eyes. "My children need me."

"And you did the right thing in coming to me. Let me take it from here. Please." It wasn't a request, but Winter was trying to be sympathetic.

Jaya shook her head slowly. "You are not their mother."

"And you're not trained in weapons or combat. And that's exactly what we might be walking into. Combat. Do you think your boys would want that for their mother?"

Her lips tightened further, all but disappearing into her mouth.

"I need you to stay out here. In the car. With the doors locked."

Jaya stood there as if she were facing off with Winter.

Finally, her shoulders caved, and she went back into the vehicle, though she didn't shut the door.

"Jaya, I'm going to go scope out the place from afar. Shut the door and lock it. This is the best chance we have of getting your sons back alive."

Jaya hesitated for a long time. She stared at the gun in Winter's hand. "Find my sons."

"I'll do everything I can."

Jaya nodded. She reached into a hidden pocket in her dress and took out an object, which she held out to Winter.

She took it without question and turned it over in her hands. An asthma inhaler.

"My son needs his medicine. This one is full."

Winter bit her lip to hold back the painful welling in her eyes. "I understand."

Jaya shut the door to the SUV and locked it.

Winter felt the pressure of Jaya's gaze as she walked closer to the cabin. She shoved the inhaler in her pocket.

Manoj and Hari—if they were inside with Erik Waller as their captor—could be in immediate danger, but she trusted that Eve and Darnell would be coming down the road soon. Normally the type to run right into danger to save the day, Winter knew better this time. Erik was coming unhinged, and she needed backup. This one had to go by the books to increase the odds of Manoj's survival.

At first glance, nothing about the cabin was remotely suspicious. But as she got closer, Winter saw that every single window appeared to be blacked out.

The scent of pine energized her as she breathed in through her nose. She paused at the tire tracks on the dusty driveway and carefully stepped over one that looked like it might've produced a decent impression. A few tiny brown dots of some substance had clearly once been a liquid, now preserved in dirt. Droplets of blood, perhaps?

It was a safe assumption that Erik's property would be covered with cameras. He seemed to have an endless supply. Likely, one would be pointed at her whether she searched for hours to find the perfect secret place to infiltrate the house or if she just walked through the front door.

Jaya's sons didn't have hours. Every moment Erik held them captive, the chances of him killing them went up.

With this in mind, and with the righteous anger of the boys' mother burning in her chest, Winter crept closer to the cabin.

Gun at the ready, she tried the knob. When it turned and swung open, her heart skipped a beat.

She paused, listening for vehicles coming up the dirt road. Nothing.

Every second matters.

Boards creaked underfoot as she moved cautiously inside. She scanned the room from left to right to help her eyes adjust to the dim light. Once she could see clearly, she left the door open behind her and stalked forward.

Nothing inside was builder-grade—custom cabinets, copper light plates, fancy Edison bulbs in the light fixtures. The place looked like it was still on the market, empty of nearly all furniture. In the main room, she found a foldable red canvas chair with a little desk in front of it.

Sitting on the desk—which was just big enough to accommodate a laptop—was an empty container of hummus and a crumpled bag that had once contained pita chips. From Black Cherry market, presumably, but not purchased recently. Not since Manoj went missing.

Careful not to touch or disturb anything, Winter conducted a quick search. There was pee in the toilet, and bandages with blood and pus in the trash bin. A twin-size blow-up mattress was laid out in the middle of the large master suite. No sheets. No pillows. No clothes or toiletries.

A white trash bag sat open in the corner of the room. Winter used the muzzle of her gun to push up the plastic and get a look at the contents. More empty containers of hummus, more pita. A large cannister that had once contained Turkish feta.

Manoj had gone missing at night after closing the Middle Eastern grocery store where he worked. Erik made a real habit of shopping there, based on the inside video surveillance footage. His diet consisted almost entirely of hummus, it appeared.

Winter moved on. In the kitchen, she smelled rot. And not any kind of rot like milk left out on a counter or dishes left to soak too long. It was the distinct smell of meat and feces—a combo she was unfortunately very familiar with, one that always portended a sense of dread.

At the back of the kitchen, Winter found a door that opened onto a lonely flight of stairs. The moment she opened it, the horrid smell intensified. Winter wrinkled her nose. Gun at the ready, she crept down the stairs.

Contrary to her expectations, there was a little more light down there. Before she could even see the room below, a small window near the ceiling drew her eye. The glass had been cracked and taped. Sunlight peeked through gaps in the shoddy repair job.

The smell of rot intensified as she stepped off the landing.

The space was small, the floor and walls made of rough concrete. Under the stairs, as she could see through the gaps, sat a cardboard box with some fabric and papers and what looked like bunny ears poking out. On the far wall, a chair lay on its side. A young man was strapped to it. An inhaler rested next to a small pool of blood coming from his chest. Even through smeared streaks of blood, she recognized his face from his photo.

Manoj Bakshi. The source of the stench of death.

"Dammit." Winter shoved her gun back into her holster, dashed forward, and crouched next to him. The inhaler matched the one in Winter's pocket, stained with bloody fingerprints.

Manoj's hands were tied together, though.

And the prints were plentiful. Possibly his little brother's? It looked like someone had tried to help him, based on the blood on the inhaler and the smears of blood on Manoj's face.

Hari. The boy was there when his older brother was

murdered. And knowing what she knew, Erik had made him watch. She wondered if he'd forced the boy to participate in some way.

Just like Justin, Erik Waller enjoyed breaking down the moral boundaries of others at least as much, if not more, than he enjoyed destroying them physically.

Twitching with anger, Winter glanced over the body one more time before narrowing her eyes at something drawn in blood near Manoj's left foot.

She didn't want to disturb the scene, so she took out her phone and snapped a picture of the sketch. Another square—like the one on the postcard. A numeral thirteen inside it. This was all in blood. Outside that was a sentence written in marker. *1 is 3 and 3 is 5, Apple Blossom!*

"Thirty-five. So if I add that to the nine, one, eight from the postcard, I get nine, one, eight, three, five?"

91835. That could be a zip code or a home address...if the square is a house.

But what were *Apple Blossom* and *Hummingbird*? Erik had capitalized the words, so she felt sure they signified demented pet names. But knowing Erik, they probably carried additional significance.

As she stared at the square, Manoj's foot twitched.

With a tiny gasp, Winter hustled back near his face—careful not to step on any bloodstains—and checked his neck for a pulse.

He had one!

She took out her phone and called 911.

She wanted to kick herself for not checking that immediately. But as she looked around the basement, she saw an area with older blood and other bodily excrements. That was where Lessner was likely killed. The smell of rot was not Manoj's body but the mess from Lessner that Erik hadn't bothered to clean up. Or had tried to, poorly, as she could faintly smell bleach too.

They'd said Lessner was killed a couple of days before being stuffed into the trunk of Manoj's car and left in the Austin PD parking lot. This basement had to be where he'd sped off to after his miraculous escape from custody. Right here in this gloomy room—with a box of what appeared to be his daughter's things—Lessner had died at Erik's hand.

As much as she hated Lessner for what he did to Noah, she couldn't help cringing. He'd already been a broken man when she met him—robbed of his higher sense of justice and morals by the trauma of losing his beloved daughter.

She didn't want to wonder, but Winter couldn't help thinking what might become of her if faced with a similar circumstance. If her husband or her grandparents were killed, and the people who did it got off with nothing but a slap on the wrist, what lengths would she go to for the sake of justice?

What do I want to do right now to Erik Waller?

She wanted to believe she'd never break the law or purposefully hurt someone for the sake of vengeance, but she could never forget the way she'd felt when she found Noah. Lying in the dirt and clutching the man she loved in her arms after knowing he'd been tortured, Winter had been ready to kill. Not just for her safety or the safety of others. She'd been ready—heart, mind, and soul—to murder Erik for what he'd done, simply because he deserved it.

A piercing scream broke the air over her.

Jaya was at the top of the stairs, her face twisted in horror. She stumbled down, perhaps recognizing the smell of death too. Or maybe her instincts as a mother propelled her.

"Jaya, wait!"

But Jaya was already lunging toward her son.

Winter caught her, arms braced as Jaya slammed against

her, sobbing, clawing, screaming his name in a chaotic mix of English and her native tongue.

"He's not dead." Winter gripped her shoulders. "Jaya. Listen to me…he's alive. He's breathing. I've called for help."

Jaya froze for half a second, her eyes wide and uncomprehending.

"An ambulance is on its way, but you have to be careful. We don't know how bad the damage is. Please…don't hurt him more."

"Manoj!" Jaya gasped again, anguish thick in her throat, but she didn't push.

Footsteps pounded above them.

"FBI!" a voice called down.

Eve. Thank God.

"Black?" Darnell shouted.

"We're in the basement. No sign of Erik, but Manoj Bakshi is down! Looks like a gunshot wound. We need EMS now!"

Jaya fought like a woman possessed, her nails digging into Winter's arms as she strained toward her son. She was small, but raw desperation gave her strength.

Winter held her back, heart pounding, not daring to loosen her grip even as footsteps thundered down the stairs —FBI, police, paramedics all crashing in at once.

The paramedics moved fast. One suctioned blood from Manoj's mouth while the other checked his chest wound and called for an intubation kit.

Jaya screamed as they began placing the tube down her son's throat. "They're choking him! What are they doing? Let me go!"

Winter tightened her grip. "They're helping him, Jaya. He can't breathe on his own…this will keep him alive. You have to trust them."

The woman's sobs turned jagged, but she stopped fighting again.

Manoj was unconscious, unresponsive, but still breathing—with help. The paramedics got the tube in, secured it, and lifted him onto a stretcher.

They were up the stairs in seconds.

Jaya sagged in Winter's arms, gutted.

One son hanging by a thread. The other still missing.

And Erik Waller—still out there, somewhere, watching it all burn.

25

Winter's knees hit the concrete before she realized she was falling. Jaya grew heavier in her arms, limp with shock, unconscious—or close to it. Winter clutched her tighter, calling her name, but the woman didn't stir.

Footsteps thundered down the stairs. A fresh wave of paramedics swarmed the space.

"She passed out." Winter studied the still woman as they eased Jaya from her grip. "She saw her son. I think the shock—"

"We've got her." They went to work, shouting vitals and oxygen levels.

Winter staggered to her feet, breath hitching, heart pounding as she climbed the stairs. The door slammed open just ahead of her, sunlight hitting like a slap. She burst into the yard in time to see the ambulance barreling down the road, sirens screaming. The urgency of them leaving gave her hope that he was still alive. For now.

She was halfway to her SUV when a voice stopped her cold. "Winter!"

Darnell.

He caught her by the arm and shoved a bottle of water into her hand. "Drink. Breathe. Or I swear I'll cuff you myself."

There wasn't time for this. "We have a ten-year-old still missing. Can't this wait?"

"We've been working together for a while now, Black." He popped the top from the water and lifted it to her lips. "You know the answer to that."

Winter ground her teeth but took a long drink. He was right. She needed to stop a moment and think everything through.

"Talk to me about the basement." Darnell wrinkled his nose. "The smell."

"Decomp, but it wasn't from Manoj." She remembered the moment she was so sure the young man was dead. Hated herself for not checking his pulse immediately. "I think it was likely Harlan Lessner. Erik killed him days ago, left him to rot."

Darnell nodded. "Just from eyeballing the blood on the floor, I'd say that's a fatal amount of blood loss for an adult. Forensics will confirm that and tell us when it was spilled."

"I found a box down there…children's things. Clothes, shoes, drawings. I bet it belonged to Lessner's daughter."

"I'll get his ex on the phone when I'm done with you to confirm. Go on."

"Jaya wouldn't give me the address unless she came. I knew it was a bad call, but I didn't have time to fight her. I should've handled it differently."

Darnell nodded slowly. "You should've. But you didn't. So let's fix it now."

Anger rushed past the regret. "Time was running out, so I—"

"Stop." But Darnell didn't appear angry. "Look. We've been working together for a while now, right?"

"Yes."

"When I first met you, I kind of wanted to beat you over the head with a newspaper for all the times you disregarded me or overstepped your bounds or failed to share pertinent information in a timely manner."

Winter blew a stray strand of black hair from her eyes. "Great."

"But I changed my mind, and I know, at least in a professional sense, exactly what was going through your head in this case."

"What's that?"

"Every second wasted is an opportunity for Erik Waller to hurt or kill the children in his custody. You know that seconds count. That's why you didn't interrogate Jaya Bakshi for the location of this cabin and just got on the road, with her riding shotgun. I get it."

What the hell? "What are you saying?"

"Officially? Nothing. Unofficially, though," Darnell took off his sunglasses to look at her directly, "I know how many lives have been saved by your pigheaded refusal to follow the rules to the letter. And by getting on the road before coercing the location out of the mother, you might've shaved twenty minutes off your arrival. You might've saved Manoj's life. Time will tell."

Winter looked up at him, silently begging the question.

"Don't expect me to say it. I will never say it." Darnell gave a mirthless chuckle and put his sunglasses back on. "I don't always understand your process, but I can't argue with your results. You probably should've refused to bring the mother. But baby steps, Black."

"Thank you, I think." She couldn't help smiling at the warm fuzzies he'd planted in her gut, even if she didn't feel like she deserved it.

A shout pulled both their attention toward the house.

Jaya.

She was being wheeled out on a gurney, strapped down, thrashing, screaming to be released. "I need to be with my son! Let me go. Please!"

Winter ran to her, Darnell on her heels.

"Jaya, stop and listen to me. They're taking good care of him. He's going to the hospital—"

"How could you let this happen?"

Winter stopped dead, not just from the words but the venom dripping from them.

"My son was here the whole time! Why did you not show me the man's picture sooner? Why did you not ask?"

How was I to know? "I'm so sorry."

"I thought the day my husband was killed would be the worst of my life. But no. In two days, I have seen my father dead on the floor and my son shot and covered in blood, hanging to life. And my baby is still out there! What are you doing to find him?"

"I'm looking. I'll never stop. I promise."

Eve appeared by the stretcher and set a hand on Jaya's shoulder. "Winter is our best chance of finding Erik Waller before he hurts your younger son. All of us are looking. We're doing everything we can."

Winter watched as Jaya's anger faded back into sorrow.

Eve met Winter's eyes—communicating her pain and sadness. Her fury at Erik. She'd worn the same eyes for Winter when she was the one in hysterics and frightened over losing her family. That was Eve's superpower. Her ability to empathize so deeply yet maintain control over herself to stay focused and do everything she could to help.

"Take me!" Jaya clutched Winter's hands. "Don't let them sedate me. Please…just take me to my car. I'll follow the ambulance."

Winter looked to the paramedic, who gave her a helpless

shake of the head. "She's stable. I recommend she see the doc, but…" He shrugged and began unbuckling the straps holding Jaya in place.

"I'll take you." Winter helped the distraught mother from the stretcher.

Winter half expected Darnell and Eve to refuse her offer, but they only nodded and helped lead them to her Pilot.

Once Jaya was safely inside the passenger seat, Darnell gripped her arm. "Call me as soon as you have her settled, got it? We have a game plan to build."

"Okay, thanks." Winter pulled away and rushed to the driver's side. She gave Eve a brief smile before shutting the door.

The moment they were on the road, Jaya urged her to hurry. "I need to see Manoj. Please take me to my cousin's house. They'll take me to the hospital and stay with me."

Winter pressed the pedal harder. "I shouldn't have brought you here. I wasn't thinking about how what we might find would affect you."

I told you to stay in the car, she almost said, but decided that would only make things worse. Jaya already knew that.

"I didn't give you a choice."

That wasn't exactly true, but Winter didn't argue. They had more important topics to discuss.

"Did you show any other homes to Erik Waller? I mean, Walter Erickson? If so, we need the addresses."

Jaya shook her head, her hands twisting together. Anxiety or guilt, Winter wasn't sure.

If she'd shown Erik other places, then the numbers 91835 were likely the address to one of them. He was slipping up.

Jaya wiped her face and pulled in a breath. "I only ever showed him that place back there."

"Did you show any other homes to him before he bought this one, any at all? Even if you didn't take him to any other homes, and he only asked about them from a website listing, anything you know could help us."

Jaya pulled out her trusty handkerchief and blew her nose. "He didn't. He didn't ask about anything or want to see anything, just this place." She shook her head, rage twisting her features into a broken snarl. "I cannot believe I did not see him for what he really is. What is wrong with me?"

Putting a hand on the woman's arm, Winter did her best to offer comfort. "Most people go their whole lives without ever being exposed to human filth as awful as that man. You're not to blame."

The word had barely left her mouth when pain lanced through her skull. She gripped the wheel tighter.

Oh, no.

Warmth dripped onto her upper lip, and she wiped it away. Blood.

Slowing the vehicle, she focused on the lines of the road to keep from crashing. Images flashed, one after the other. Petals. White and pink. Apple blossoms. Inhaling deeply, she could almost smell them.

"Are you okay?" Jaya's voice seemed to be coming from far away.

Fighting against the vision, Winter was deeply grateful when the pain receded and her vision cleared. She wiped her hand on her pants. "I'm fine. Just stressed."

Thankfully, the mother was too distraught over her children to focus on Winter's distress.

"There." Jaya pointed toward the next road. "That's the way to my cousin's house."

Winter glanced at Jaya. "I can take you to the hospital."

"No. I want to be with my family, please. They'll help me get to the hospital and will stay with me." She turned dark eyes Winter's way. "While you find my Hari."

The plan made sense.

Winter kept her hands at nine and three, knuckles white, gripping the wheel like she was driving through a blizzard. The only words Jaya muttered were to give Winter directions to her cousin's house.

When she pulled into the driveway, next to a blue Toyota Corolla, she squeezed Jaya's hand. "I'll be praying for Manoj while I find Hari."

And kill the bastard who took him.

Jaya's expression softened, and tears pooled in her eyes. "Thank you, Winter. For the prayer and for bringing my baby back to me."

She was out of the SUV a second later, running toward the front door.

Please, God, let both of this kind woman's children survive.

If Manoj didn't pull through, if Erik killed Hari, Jaya would never recover. Winter might not either.

She had to stop this monster once and for all.

26

Fueled by anger and adrenaline, Winter sped toward her office. Ariel would be there, and she needed help finding answers. Houses zipped by in the background as she raced down one street and then another, unable to concentrate on anything but her vision and her fury.

You don't want to start a manhunt with those emotions steering the train.

She thought about the vision she'd experienced. Erik had called her "Apple Blossom" on the basement floor. This was no coincidence.

Unfortunately, she hadn't seen anything else. Nothing to direct her someplace specific. That was where Ariel would come in.

She turned a corner, and her squealing tires drew the attention of an older couple carrying groceries from their car.

Winter eased back on the accelerator.

Your name isn't Emma Last so don't drive like her.

Thinking of the "super girl" club's third member, Winter slowed even more, to just over the speed limit. The D.C.

Violent Crime Unit's agent had a habit of rushing in ahead of any angels that might be watching. Winter Black and Autumn Trent had the same tendencies.

Driving slowly was difficult at the moment. She needed to save a ten-year-old boy. But she took the next corner at a modest speed.

Erik wanted to replace Justin, and maybe he has. Maybe he's worse than the worst monster I've ever known. Justin. But that just means he'll get stomped down even harder when I do stop him.

Her anger threatened to boil over, and she nearly sideswiped a car pulling off the curb without signaling.

Screeching to a stop and slamming a hand on the steering wheel, Winter roared and cursed. Once the other car had driven down the street, she pulled into the vacated space and shut off her engine.

Winter's phone was in her hand a second later. She tapped Noah's number.

He picked up on the first ring. "Where are you? I can be there in five minutes. Yesterday, if you really need me."

"I do. Really need you. Erik tried to kill Jaya's oldest son. He's at the hospital. And he's kidnapped her youngest. I just left Jaya with her cousin. All I can think about is how much I want to watch his skin blister off his bones."

Noah's slow whistle came through the phone like a cool breeze against her ear. "Maybe you need to step away. Let the D&E Team handle this."

"The who now?"

"Darnell and Eve."

She laughed out loud, enjoying the pleasure of knowing her husband was still the man she'd met as a newly minted FBI agent. He was still the man who'd slept on her hotel room floor like a guard dog, when Justin had been haunting them both anew.

"You're right, babe. But Erik won't stop until he gets what he wants. Me. And I'm close to figuring out where he is now."

"So tell the cops. Or tell me, and I'll tell them. Don't you dare rush after him on your own."

She scoffed. "As if I'd do that and leave you to worry about me."

Except I really want to.

"I can hear you thinking, Winter. Where are we going?"

Stifling the urge to hang up, she took a deep breath and remembered the day she first put on a badge. The day she met Aiden Parrish and the other agents who would form her FBI family. She remembered meeting Autumn Trent, the best friend she'd ever made.

Braced by those memories, Winter got her husband up to date on the cabin, how she'd found it, and what she thought was happening next. And she mentioned the clue she'd found in the basement, too, near Manoj's unconscious body. "Just like the ones on that postcard we found, and with numbers again. Different ones. And another pet name." Saying *pet name* made Winter gag a little.

"So he wrote ninety-one and a riddle on the postcard."

"Yes, the riddle was a spider. We can thank Gramma Beth. So if we go with eight legs, the numbers are nine, one, eight from the first clue. And 'hummingbird' was capitalized."

Noah cursed quietly. "This guy and his damn games and puzzles. What the hell are we supposed to do with that?"

"Well, the second clue was three and five with 'apple blossom' written like a nickname."

"This fucking guy."

"And when I was driving Jaya earlier, I had a vision of apple blossoms. Lots of them."

"Shit…you okay?" The concern was clear in his voice. He knew how bad her visions could be.

"Yeah. It was small, thank goodness, with only the images of the flowers."

He exhaled. "Good. Any idea what they represent?"

"I think it's a location." A terrible thought occurred to Winter. "What if Jaya knows the location and lied to me?"

"What?" Noah sounded bewildered. "Why on earth would she do that? Don't tell me she's secretly in cahoots with Erik."

"She thinks we're too slow, too incompetent. She was furious with me for not showing her Erik's photo sooner." Winter rubbed her temples. "I think she knows where Erik's taken Hari, and she's planning to go rescue him by herself."

"So do we follow her every move until she takes us there? Grabbing my keys now." She could hear him moving around.

"Could it be an address, 91835, and the words could be street names?"

"Apple Blossom Place or Hummingbird Road?" Noah huffed, beyond annoyed. "No streets I've ever heard of. A zip code?"

"We'll figure it out. I'm at the office."

"Perfect. I don't have time to almost lose you again, Winter. I'm on my way there. Besides, Erik's the reason I only have nine fingers, and I'm looking forward to kicking his ass with eight of them tied behind my back."

The guard dog was out.

"Sounds good. Call the D&E Team and let them know I'm going to figure this out by the time you get here." With that, Winter hung up and charged through the door of her office, beelining to Ariel's desk. "I know where he is."

"You what? Who? Erik?" Ariel popped up from her chair as Winter reached her.

Winter could hardly tell her she'd had a vision of a sea of tiny white-and-pink flowers in bloom. "Well, I don't know where Erik is, but we can find him. Sit! Sit back down."

Ariel did as ordered and set her fingers on her keyboard, at the ready.

Winter caught her up on everything at the cabin, the Bakshi boys' statuses, and all the clues from Erik. "I believe he has Hari somewhere that has something to do with this information." She wrote it all down.

918 and 35 or 91835.

Hummingbird.

Apple Blossom.

Ariel's fingers flew over the keyboard. "Well, 918 is an area code in Oklahoma. No-go there. 91835 is not a zip code anywhere. There is no 91835 Apple Blossom Road, Lane, Place, Drive, or Avenue in Texas. Or 91835 Hummingbird Road, Place—"

"I get it, Ariel." Winter paced behind her, spying over her shoulders every thirty seconds or so. "Does Texas have any apple orchards that are…of note? Or close?"

"We sure do. Medina is known as the Apple Capital of Texas, and other areas in Hill Country have orchards, one near Lubbock. There's Love Creek Orchard, Apple Valley Orchard, and The Apple Conservatory—"

"Any called 'apple blossom' specifically? Do you need water?" Winter took off for the fridge and was back in a flash with two water bottles. She set one next to Ariel's pencil holder.

"Thank you kindly." Ariel uncapped it and took a quick sip. "Okay, um, apple blossom…" She let out a little squeal.

"What?" Winter was literally breathing down Ariel's neck, reading over her shoulder. "Apple Blossom Estates. An abandoned neighborhood built too deep into a flood plain back in 2015. All the houses are vacant. That's where Erik's hiding!"

"You mean that's where he might be *waiting*." Ariel shot her a worried look. "For you, Boss."

Winter didn't like hearing those words, but they were true.

"It says that only a handful of homes are even habitable out of one hundred. But the division was a multimillion-dollar deal that went up in smoke, well, water, before most of the homes were even purchased. A flood." Winter bit a nail, a newly forming habit thanks to Erik. "It's a trap, and if the place is abandoned, he's had plenty of time to do whatever he needs to make that trap deadly."

"How are we supposed to find which house he's in anyway? Go door to door like the Girl Scouts?" Ariel turned, her head cocked.

"My guess is he's in the one at 91835 Hummingbird Road, Street, Lane, or whatever. He's losing his game, and his clues are getting weak. Can you pull up a schematic of the estates? Is it possible to find that online?"

Ariel snorted. "Is it possible?"

Within a minute, she'd found a plan of the estates. And right there, among a hundred or more houses, was a square marked *35* in Apple Blossom Estates—they had a location of the entire development, and that house could be the one Erik was in. They knew how to get to the home. The *918* and *Hummingbird* part of this riddle would have to fall into place once they got there.

Winter spotted Noah through the front window of her office, and she grabbed her bag. It was time to go save Hari Bakshi and stop Erik Waller for good.

27

Behind the wheel of the Pilot, Winter stared straight ahead, speeding them down the highway outside of Austin proper. She could feel Noah watching her, waiting for the answer she knew she would give.

"Darlin', talk to me."

"We're going to save Jaya's son, whatever that takes." She nodded at the duffel on his lap. "What's in your bag of tricks?"

He patted the bag. "Wire cutters, in case he's rigged up trip wires around the property. Zip ties for when we find his ass."

"Assuming ass is alive to be zip-tied."

He turned in his seat to face her fully. "Winter, we're going in with the intent of saving a life, not taking one. I need to know we're on the same page." He reached out to grip her knee.

She fought back the anger that threatened to simmer up again. "Thanks for bringing the extra-large zip ties. I plan to use that entire pack to restrain him."

Noah's laugh was warm and welcome and helped dispel

her rage even more. "You and me both have a bone to pick with our boy. I'm looking forward to making him squirm. Really want to get him under my *thumb*, you know."

"Dammit, Noah." Winter smacked her hand against his chest, and they shared a laugh as the vehicle raced along.

"I need to let Eve know where we're heading."

Winter bit her lower lip. "Are you sure? What if I'm wrong about the location?"

"What if you're right?"

She blew out a long breath. "Yeah…call in all the troops, and if I'm wrong…" She shrugged.

She wasn't wrong. She could feel it.

Noah tapped Eve's contact. The line rang until her voicemail answered.

Shit.

Noah left a message for her to return his call urgently. "I'll send her the address too."

As he typed, she gestured to the duffel. "What else?"

"Basic trauma kit with saline, coagulant, and bandages. We have two splints, so only one broken bone for each of us, deal?"

That was the Marine in him, preparing for deployment and every eventuality he could foresee. "Deal. And I get to break his arm, his right arm. You can have the other one or a leg."

Noah's gape-mouthed stare had her laughing again. He finally joined in, shaking his head and gripping her knee tightly.

She placed her hand over his, careful to avoid the area near his missing digit. As they approached the abandoned development, Winter slowed and their laughter died.

All sound in her vehicle faded away as they took in the scope of the disaster that had befallen Apple Blossom Estates. The remains of two brick subdivision signs stood like ancient ruins framing the street. They were both partially knocked over, with none of the actual signage still visible. Flood debris mounded against the bases, and vines crawled across the fallen bricks scattered nearby.

The roadway entering the neighborhood was likewise littered with debris, much of which might've once been parts of the houses themselves. The first several houses along the entry road were still standing, in various states of ruin.

Winter could see others missing roofs or with nothing but a crumbled chimney stack to mark their footprint. But where the houses were decaying, the apple trees thrived. Blossoming. The fragrant smell was impossible to miss. It was such a strange contrast, given the broken-down state of the area.

She rolled them forward, circling a pile of tree limbs and splintered bits of wood.

Noah stiffened in his seat and ran a hand over his brow. "Wish we had an EOD disruptor in this vehicle."

"You think Erik has that kind of ordnance?"

"I think we'd be dumb to ignore the possibility of explosives. Just keep us clear of any trash piles, okay? I'll keep a lookout for broken-up parts on the street."

She drove along, stopping at the first intersection and checking in every direction. The rage that'd gotten them there was now doing battle with anxiety.

Winter scanned every structure she could see, looking for the slightest glint or reflected light. Noah's reference to the hazards of warfare brought to mind another image. She looked from window to window in all the nearest buildings. Each window, each shadowy nook, could hide Erik with a rifle and scope. The hairs on her arms and neck stood up.

Noah had a printout of the division on his lap, but they were both mostly watching the roadway and everything else.

He gestured to the map. "Looks like we drive through

three more intersections, go right, and it'll be the last house on that block on the right."

She drove forward on the two-lane street that rose in a shallow incline. Heaps and drifts of debris spread across what had once been lawns and gardens. Some spilled into the street and sat mounded against the curbs.

"There's a street called Robin Place." Noah read the rusty sign out loud. "And there's Bluejay, coming up. Something tells me…"

The piles were smaller after they continued forward. Winter scanned the area, half expecting a hole to appear in the glass at any moment, as a rifle shot ended the life she'd built from the ashes of her past.

They passed Bluejay Way. "We're sitting ducks out here. He could be in any of these places watching us."

"I know." Noah gave her arm a squeeze. "I'm looking too. Just keep going."

The homes were getting bigger, these the least damaged so far. And they had the widest stretches of yard between them.

Sure enough, the third road—and the one their home was on, if she'd gotten his clues right—was Hummingbird Lane. "Here we go."

She turned right. A dozen homes stood between them and their destination, starting with 900 Hummingbird Lane on the right side of the roadway. It was one long road and had a mild incline.

As Winter took a wide circle around a mound of branches on their right to pull over about four houses down from 918, she spotted a hint of blue between some overgrown shrubs in the side yard between the two homes to her right.

"Shit, she did lie to us. Dammit!" Winter parked the car down from where the blue Toyota Corolla sat. "Jaya's cousin had a car just like that one in their driveway. She knew exactly where he was going all along."

"Desperate people do desperate things," Noah murmured.

Yeah, especially desperate mothers. Very few things were fiercer.

"Hari's in there, and Jaya is either in the house, too, or somewhere close. But I bet Erik has her."

Noah nodded. "She ran straight into the cabin for her sons, right?"

"Right, so I imagine she'd do the same here." Winter exhaled most of the air in her lungs, willing her growing anxiety to exit with it. "Erik's going to do it all over again."

"Do what?"

"He's going to force me to make a choice, like Justin did."

Noah cupped the back of her neck, his thumb moving in slow, steady circles—just enough to ease the tightness there. Just enough to say he was with her. "Hey, this won't be like the Stewarts. I promise."

Winter folded forward slightly, her arms wrapping around her middle—not to comfort herself, but to hold something in. A scream. A sob. A memory.

She could still feel their necks snapping beneath her hands. Still hear the way the children had screamed for their parents, not understanding what was happening—only that it was happening because of her. Justin's voice, calm and gleeful in her ear.

Though Subject A is the de facto leader...

The promise that if she obeyed, the kids would live. And the truth that followed.

Her breath caught in her throat.

This wasn't just another criminal. Not just another monster.

This was a disciple of the very darkness that had hollowed her out. And she was about to walk into his world.

Again.

Regret coursed through her veins like a river, no matter how many times she reminded herself she'd been manipulated. Held at gunpoint.

...a sense of empathy and responsibility for Subject A may have been contributing psychological factors in Subject B's cooperation.

Forced to choose between one life or four.

But she couldn't do it again. She *would not* be made to take another life while a child—or anyone—watched.

Except the gun had been aimed at a boy's head. At Timothy Stewart's head. And she'd had no choice.

What if Erik has a gun on Hari?

What then?

Timothy Stewart had lived, even as his family was slaughtered in front of him. He'd survived.

So had she…mostly.

And so had Justin—the one who orchestrated every sick second of it inside that camper. The one Erik now worshiped.

Noah, as usual, seemed to know exactly what she was thinking. "Winter? Darlin', you can't change what happened, and you couldn't have done anything to stop Justin at the time. You were drugged, and—"

"I know!" More regret surged sharp and hot, and she snatched his hand between hers, pressing her lips to the exposed flesh between the bandage. "I'm sorry I yelled."

"It's okay. But it's not the same. He didn't know Jaya would go rogue and come here."

"Didn't he?" Winter desperately wished that was true. "He mentioned these estates to her. He showed interest so that she would remember it. He planned this whole thing."

Winter unbuckled her seat belt and reached for her pistol under her seat. She checked that it was loaded and set the safety.

"This is a dangerous infil operation with now two potential hostages and a hostile element. And we don't know for sure he knows we're coming."

"He's waiting and watching, because that's what Justin would do. Erik wants to replace him in every way. Hari's already lost his grandfather, and he believes his older brother's dead. Now his mother is likely in there, awaiting the same fate. He's trying to replicate what Justin did with Timothy Stewart."

As she spoke, Noah's features clouded over. He'd survived being stabbed when Timothy was fully under Justin's sway.

Even though that little boy's mind, heart, and hands were manipulated by a psychopath, he was the one who stabbed the knife into Noah.

"We have to save Hari. Before he's forced to watch his mother die in front of him. Hell, Erik could even force him to commit the act himself. He'd find some way to do it, just like Justin did."

Noah gripped the strap of the duffel bag so tightly she thought he might rip it in half. "Let's go."

Winter reached across the console, careful to take his right hand—his good hand—into hers. She didn't want to risk jostling the left, where the bandage still wrapped around his missing finger like a ghost of what he'd lost.

Because of me.

"I need to tell you something." Though she tried to be strong, her voice was thick with emotion.

Noah stilled. His eyes searched hers. "What, darlin'?"

"I love you." She kissed his fingers, one by one. "More than I've ever been able to say. You've stood by me through every impossible moment. Every time I shut you out, every time I let the job pull me too far under…you stayed. You believed in me."

He squeezed her fingers gently, his good hand warm and

steady in hers. "Of course I do." His left came up to brush away a fallen tear.

She pulled in a breath that hurt and leaned over the console to kiss him. She wanted to stop time right then, let this moment linger for eternity.

She couldn't. Too much was at stake.

"Then believe in me one more time."

Metal clicked.

"What the hell?" Noah looked down just as she snapped the cuff around his right wrist and looped the second through the steering wheel.

"Winter…no! What are you doing?" He yanked at it, eyes wide with disbelief and betrayal.

She grabbed his left arm when he reached for her, trying to keep him from hurting himself more. Tears spilled freely as she begged him to understand. "I can't lose you, Noah. I can't watch you bleed again. I can't watch you die."

He twisted and fought, grabbing at her shirt, her vest, her hair. "No! Don't do this. You can't leave me here like this!"

But she had to. There was no other choice.

"I love you." Slipping from the SUV, Winter grabbed her gun. "I'll come back." Before she could change her mind, she slammed the door.

"No! Stop! Wait for backup at least!"

Noah's voice chased her across the broken concrete. Behind her, the Pilot rocked as he pounded his fist on the steering wheel. He kicked at the dashboard, over and over, causing the whole SUV to shake.

He was going to hurt himself. She turned to go back, to tell him to stop, to let him come with her…

A scream.

Raw. Piercing. Human.

Winter didn't look back.

She ran toward the house.

28

Hari sat on a bed, scrunched up in the corner like a wad of paper, eyes squeezed shut. He gripped the edge of the mattress so hard his fingers hurt, but he didn't loosen them. Not even as he prayed to be saved.

They'd come, wouldn't they? The police and FBI would help him. They had to.

He just had to wait. Sit still. Be brave.

Don't cry.

Erik laughed like he'd done all day, that awful sound scraping against Hari's nerves like a fork on a plate.

He hated that laugh. Hated that voice. Hated how Erik said his name wrong on purpose.

"Open your eyes, Harry."

Hari shook his head hard and pressed his hands over his ears. If he didn't look at him, the gun might go away. If he didn't move, Erik might forget he was there.

The slap came fast.

His face snapped sideways, and the scream tore out of him before he could stop it. His cheek burned like it had touched fire. He reached up and felt the wet.

Blood.

His eyes opened. He didn't want them to, but fear forced him to see what would happen next.

Erik stood over him, smiling like he was proud. Like he'd won.

Hari's hands trembled as he stared at the red on his fingers. "I hate you."

"Hey now, is that any way to talk to your new BFF, bro? We're gonna be so good together."

"Screw you."

The words barely came out, but they were loud enough that Erik lifted the gun like he might hit him with it.

Hari flinched before he could stop the movement. He wanted to be brave, but he was only ten.

"You wanna watch that mouth. It'll get knocked off your face if you're not careful." He reached to the nightstand beside the bed for a plastic cup he'd been sipping from earlier. "Want some supercharged fruit punch? My own recipe."

Hari was thirsty and hungry. But mostly, he was terrified, and he didn't trust anything the deranged man said.

"Supercharged" probably meant poisoned or full of drugs. Hari shook his head and looked out the glass balcony door. He couldn't see much outside except trees. "I want to go home. Why are you doing this?"

Erik laughed. "It's, like, fate. I'm gonna be so much better than Justin."

Nothing this stupid man said made sense. "Than who?"

After a pause, Erik swallowed a big gulp from the juice. "You've never heard of Justin Black? That makes me sad. But don't worry, little bro. We're gonna have plenty of time to get acquainted."

Hari wondered if the time had come to try to escape. He wanted so badly to go home, to be anywhere but in this smelly old house. He wanted to run away from Erik and his gun. Hari's cheek burned where he'd hit him. The bleeding had stopped, but it stung when his hand brushed against the torn skin.

Erik was staring at the ceiling now, a big smile on his face when a scream shattered the stillness.

Hari flinched and curled into a ball again.

Another scream echoed down the hallway like it had come from the stairs. Maybe it had. Maybe someone was here? This Justin person?

Erik moved to the door and pressed his ear against it, eyes dancing. "Ohhh yeah. I think I hear a mouse on the stairs." He yanked out a hunk of wood from under the door and ran out into the hall.

More screaming. Hari's mother. Her voice was thunder and fire and heartbreak all at the same time. She was here.

Hari jumped up, heart thudding against his ribs. He wanted to run to her, but Erik came barreling back into the room, dragging someone behind him.

Maata.

She fell to her knees. Her shoe was torn. Blood seeped from her foot. She was hurt.

"Maata! What did he do? What happened?"

She wrapped him in a hug, and they huddled together. The smell of her hair was something Hari thought he would never experience again. He held her tight, finally knowing a moment of safety and comfort after being so afraid.

Tears rained down his forehead as his mother shook with sobs. "Hari, I have you. You are safe now. I am here."

Erik slammed the door shut and jammed a wooden latch into place across the door, barricading them all inside. His laugh came loud and booming above them. "That's right. Mommy's here, little bro." His voice went low and evil again. "For now. Almost time for you to level up."

Looking from under his mother's arm, Hari watched Erik pacing around the room with his gun. He took a pill bottle out of his pocket and twisted the top off with his teeth. Erik looked into the bottle. "Dang."

He threw his head back and swallowed whatever was in there, tossing the empty container away.

Humming, he walked over to where Hari and his mom sat on the mattress, their backs against the wall. He grabbed Hari's arm, and Maata swung a fist, hitting Erik in the balls, but only hard enough to make him mad.

"Bitch! Did I give consent? I don't think I did." He grabbed Maata by her hair and pulled her away.

Hari reached for her, but Erik kicked him in the stomach, knocking the air out of him. His chest burned as he sucked in a breath, desperate to help Maata. She needed him, and he wasn't going to let Erik get away with hurting her too.

He finally got his wind again and stood up. Maata was on her knees, sobbing, with Erik's gun pointed at her head. "Little bro, my patience is about done. The cops are probably on their way, so we're going to make them happy. Go out the door."

"No! Let Maata go and let me go. I won't help you!"

Maata screamed as Erik hauled her up by her hair and stuck the gun under her chin. "Okay. Then you get to see Mama's brains and probably wear some of them too. Deal?"

"No…please. Let us go."

His pupils were huge, wild, like a cat stalking a bird. Erik smiled, showing Hari his teeth. "Countdown has started, little bro. If you're gonna level up, it's gotta be now. Get out there." He nodded toward the glass doors and jammed his gun under Maata's chin harder, making her cry out.

Hari's feet stayed rooted in place. He couldn't move. Couldn't think.

"Go, Hari." Tears poured down Maata's face, but she managed a little smile. "Do what he says. It will be okay."

Deep in his gut, Hari knew it was a lie.

But what could he do?

With one last glance at his mother, Hari turned to the balcony and whatever fate awaited him there.

29

Winter crouched beside the front door, weapon ready. The house loomed silent but for the screams and manic yells coming down from the second floor. She rose to her feet and tested the knob. Locked.

She stepped back and kicked once, hard. The wood splintered, and the door gave way, crashing open into darkness.

Now she stood with her back to the gaping frame, breath quickening, heart pounding. Not one scream—several. They echoed from somewhere above, slicing through the silence like knives. Desperate. Terrified. Real.

She didn't know which one was Jaya's. Or Hari's. Or Erik's. But they were up there. All of them.

And she couldn't wait

From a key hook on the wall to her left hung two sets of keys. Each set had a tag—one with Erik's name and the other with hers. *Hers.* Like this was all part of some twisted plan, as if he truly believed she belonged to him. The sight made her stomach turn.

She moved past them, deeper into the house. Every step

was a balance between instinct and control. Erik was clever, and she couldn't afford to rush. Not now. Not with people's lives at stake.

No backup was coming. Not in time, at least. She'd cuffed the man she loved to a steering wheel to make sure of that. This fight was hers.

Another scream tore down the stairs. Sharper. Closer.

Her pulse kicked up, and she raised her weapon in one hand, flashlight in the other. Her breath came short, sharp, too loud in the still air of the ruined house. Dim light filtered through cracks in the boarded-up windows. Water stains climbed the walls like veins.

Every part of her body was wired, tight with tension. She remembered what it was like to walk into danger like this before—except she usually had backup. A team at her back. But this? This was personal.

The entry hall yawned in front of her. Shadows stretched like claws. She passed the kitchen, gaze sweeping the dark spaces, alert for movement. Any flicker. Any sound. Every creak beneath her boots sounded like a shout.

Ahead, the stairs loomed. Narrow. Covered in dust. Waiting.

She took one step…and froze.

Her ankle had nudged something.

Swinging the flashlight low, she cursed under her breath. A net of wires crisscrossed the hall, tight as piano strings. Thin, sharp, and wound through eyehooks and nails. Some of them stretched up toward the ceiling, disappearing into cracks she couldn't see through.

Jaya had made it through this. Or almost. Was that why she'd screamed? Had she set something off?

Winter swallowed hard. She couldn't think about that now.

One foot forward. Then another.

She moved like a dancer on a minefield. Each motion deliberate. Her heart pounded so loud. it was like a second pulse in her neck. The wires shimmered in the beam of her light. Some glinted where the coating had worn away—metal ready to bite.

Each wire avoided felt like a small victory. But there was no time to celebrate. Only forward.

She made it to the stairs. Listened.

Voices. Muffled. More yelling. She recognized one.

Erik.

The hairs on the back of her neck prickled.

As she climbed, a distant wail threaded its way through the pounding in her ears. Sirens. Growing louder. Help was coming but not fast enough.

The vest shifted against her chest, heavy and hot. Her thighs burned. But the pain grounded her. Kept her from thinking too far ahead.

She tried not to think of Noah, alone and helpless in the car. Of what this would do to him if she didn't come back. If she failed. Again.

The second floor opened into a hallway. A faded runner stretched down the middle, spotted and warped. Doors lined both sides. At the far end, one door stood shut. Thick. Solid.

From behind it…shouting. Crying.

Jaya and Hari. And Erik.

Winter moved forward, stepping around something bulky. She crouched to check it—towels. Blood-soaked. Shoved aside to reveal a spiked plank of wood beneath.

A trap.

Her jaw clenched. Her gut churned.

She moved forward, scanning every inch of space. Every inch of the hallway demanded her attention. No rugs. No furniture. Nothing to suggest comfort or life. Just bare, stained wood beneath her boots—worn down by time and rotted dreams.

To her left, the bathroom yawned open, a dark mouth ready to swallow her whole.

She stepped past it and cursed at the tug at her ankle. Before she could step back, the wire snapped.

Her instincts surged. Before her brain even registered what had happened, her body twisted. She dropped low, bracing.

Boom.

The gun fired from somewhere above or behind. The blast hit her vest square in the ribs, knocking her sideways. Air fled her lungs. The pain was massive, a tidal wave of pressure that made her vision go white for a moment.

She slammed to the ground. Hands. Knees. Face inches from the floor.

Still breathing.

Still alive.

The vest had held.

But God, it hurt.

Her side screamed. Every breath lit up the bruises already blooming beneath the Kevlar. She bit her lip to keep from crying out.

She rolled to her knees, hand bracing against the wall. She was moving again within seconds, dragging herself upright with a grunt.

Every inch of her body seemed to be burning, but her focus never wavered.

The door at the end of the hall stayed shut.

But not for long.

She'd made it this far. Through the wires. The stairs. The trap.

Winter wasn't stopping now.

Not until she reached them.
Not until she ended this.

30

Noah yanked against the cuff again, his wrist raw, heart pounding as he cursed his wife for the hundredth time in the past few minutes. The moment Winter stepped out of the SUV and shut the door behind her, he'd known. Known she wasn't going to wait. Known she intended to end this on her own.

He'd never loved and hated anyone more in his life.

Sirens crept through the cracked window, faint at first, then louder—wailing like a chorus of ghosts as they descended on Apple Blossom Estates. Noah turned as much as he could to watch the flashing lights flickering through the wreckage of the overgrown development. It should have comforted him.

It didn't.

He was trapped. Again. Powerless to protect the woman he loved.

Again.

The driver's side door opened, and Noah jerked, gun halfway raised before he registered the figure standing there.

Eve.

She looked down at him, her brows pulled tight. "Jesus, she really cuffed you."

Noah didn't answer.

"I'm not unlocking you." She flashed him a brittle smile, already anticipating the argument. "You'd rush in without a plan, and we both know it."

"You think I care about plans right now?"

"I think you care about her. And if you do, you'll sit still until we know what we're dealing with."

Noah already knew what they were dealing with. And he didn't like it one bit.

Voices outside rose in a chorus of movement and preparation. SWAT. Bomb Squad. Local PD. Agents and techs and medics. All buzzing around the house, but no one going inside. Not yet.

SSA Falkner's voice echoed across the cracked pavement, amplified through a megaphone. "Erik Waller, we're here to help you. Come back to the window. Let's talk."

Noah strained against the steering wheel, trying to see. Instead of Erik, he caught a glimpse…shit. It was Hari, standing on the balcony over the front door. His arms wrapped tight around himself. Something around his neck—a collar.

Noah's breath left his body. Relief. Horror. Both.

The boy was alive.

But not safe.

Screams followed, then laughter—wild and frenzied. Erik.

A shotgun blast tore through the air. Noah flinched.

"Winter." He slammed his fist against the steering wheel, no longer caring how much it hurt his fucking hand. "Dammit, Eve! I have to go in!"

Her hand shot out to stop him. "You think I don't want to? She's my friend too. But we do this smart. He's watching, probably from a scope. We rush the house, he kills someone. Or makes Winter do it."

Noah sagged back in his seat. Sweat rolled down the side of his face.

She was right.

He could hear them working. A drone lifting into the air. Radio chatter about thermal imaging, layout clearances, pressure sensors. It was the right process.

But it wasn't fast enough.

Falkner kept talking, steady and calm. "We just want to help, Erik. You have the power to decide how this ends. Let us help Hari. Let us help his mother."

No response.

Hari moved. A shuffle on the balcony. The collar glinted in the sunlight.

Noah's stomach twisted.

"Is that thing a bomb?" The words were gravel in his throat.

Eve didn't answer immediately, only nodded once. "Could be. And that's why we wait. Until we're sure."

Noah couldn't wait anymore. "You have to let me go. I can help her."

"I said no."

"I've cleared houses in war zones. I know traps. I know how to move. Let me go in, Eve."

"And if you trip something and get her killed? Or that kid? You willing to carry that?"

"She's already in there. You think I'm not already carrying it?"

Eve cursed softly and turned her back, muttering into her radio. Noah watched her shoulders tighten. Heard words like *collar*, *hostage*, *confirmed*.

He didn't stop pleading.

"Please. She went in because she thought it was the only

way. Because she thought it would save me. Don't make that sacrifice for nothing. Don't let her do this alone."

Eve didn't answer. Didn't move.

Until she did.

She turned back to the cab, pulled out a key, and unlocked the cuff with one sharp click.

"You go in behind SWAT." Her voice was low and furious. "And you don't play hero. You help us find her. You support her. You stay alive. You do not make this worse."

Noah rubbed his wrist, sliding out of the Pilot. "I'll bring them all out. I swear."

Eve stepped back, already radioing Falkner. "We've got movement. Stand by."

Noah didn't wait.

He ran.

Toward the house.

Toward Winter.

Toward whatever hell waited behind that door.

31

Winter crouched behind the doorframe, ears still ringing from the blast that had knocked her off her feet. Her ribs ached with every breath, the bruising beneath her vest spreading like fire across her side.

She checked the floor carefully, making sure there wasn't another trap. As she rose to her feet, she heard it. Footsteps downstairs. Heavy. Familiar.

Not Erik. Her heart skipped.

She crept toward the stairs, pausing just before the top step, gun gripped tightly in both hands. Several silhouettes moved below, one edging cautiously toward the steps.

Noah.

She nearly collapsed with relief—but urgency propelled her forward. She had to stop him before he was hurt.

"Trip wires! Bottom of the stairs and up here too!" Her whisper carried like a bullet.

Noah looked up, saw her, and nodded once. His expression morphed from anger to relief and back again, and she knew that, if they both survived this mess, she had some explaining to do later. But not right now.

He froze, waiting for her cue. She backed up toward the hallway, motioning with two fingers for him to wait until she cleared the landing.

Back in front of the door, she resumed her position just as Erik let out another cackling laugh. The door rattled in its frame, and thuds sounded from inside—he was throwing something. Or someone.

Jaya's scream ripped through the wood.

Winter raised her weapon again, finger steady on the trigger.

Behind her, the soft scuffle of Noah's boots told her he'd made it safely past the wires. He was almost there.

But then—

The door creaked.

Not open yet. Just the sound of pressure, the hinge flexing. There was a *pop*. Then another.

Red smoke billowed into the hallway, and Winter barely had time to shout a warning before she was enveloped in it. Her eyes seared. Her nose filled with acid.

Too late.

She felt Erik's presence an instant before he struck. A fist to her gut bent her in half, and the gun was yanked from her grip. She fell back coughing, vision swimming from the pepper spray.

Noah's voice—raw, furious—called her name.

She tried to speak. To warn him.

Another scream from Jaya.

Noah's thundering footsteps gave her a moment of hope before Erik grabbed her by the hair and pulled her through the doorway. He shot more pepper spray rounds into the hall and slammed the door shut.

A loud *clomp* of wood falling into place told Winter he'd barricaded them in somehow. She struggled to her knees, sucking in air as best she could and blinking, knowing that swiping at her eyes would only make the pepper spray worse. All she could see were tear-streaked images of dirty carpet.

Every breath was like pulling air through sludge. She'd get a taste of oxygen, just enough to cough and sputter again.

And through it all, Erik Waller's sinister laughter rang out, a cackling, taunting soundtrack to her distress.

Winter crawled blindly, trying to locate her weapon.

"Don't bother, baby. I got your gun right here."

She flailed her arms in front of her, shaking her head. Winter wanted to wipe her eyes, but her hands and clothing were all coated in the pepper spray.

Water, saline. I need Noah's first aid kit, dammit!

Noah pounded on the door, trying to break in.

"Lover boy needs to chill." He swallowed a laugh as Winter finally worked up enough tears to wash some of the pepper from her stinging eyes. She got some relief, but only enough to see Erik, holding her gun in one hand while rubbing his groin with the other.

"You piece of shit." She lunged for him, and he swung the gun at her head, knocking her sideways. With another laugh, he grabbed her by the hair again. She kicked out, but he dodged, and her foot hit nothing but air.

Winter reached for the hand tangled in her hair. She got a grip on it, but he slammed the gun against her wrists until she let go.

Noah's pounding increased. But the heavy wooden latch across the door was doing its job. Erik flung Winter onto the bed, and she landed next to a body. She turned to find a bloodied but still breathing Jaya huddling against the wall.

Finally able to take in a full breath, she fought to relax and get her bearings. Fighting blind would only injure her more.

At last, the mist was settling, and Winter took in the room.

They were on a bed tucked into the corner. The French doors to the balcony were on the wall in front of them. An empty closet stood open next to the barricaded door. A heavy beam of wood had been laid across the entrance, held in place with metal brackets.

The doorframe had been reinforced on this side, too, with additional layers of wood and new, heavy hinges.

Erik stood in the center of the room, snickering and running a finger under his nose. Winter's gun was still in his hand. It raised the question, where was his own gun? He jerked his head toward the door as Noah's weight rattled it in its frame.

"You want to tell him to knock it off? I'm getting tired of all that noise. That door isn't opening unless I want it to."

Winter coughed hard, her lungs straining against the lingering effects of the pepper spray.

You've never had an angry Marine try to get in here before, Erik. That door is coming down.

He paced back and forth in front of the bed, the hand holding her gun twitching against his leg. Noah slammed against the door again, and Erik spun, shooting at it twice.

A loud grunt came from the other side, and Winter flew at Erik. The gun came around, crashing into her shoulder.

Movement sounded from the hallway, followed by Noah's angry curses. Eve was out there with him now, and they had a first aid kit. He'd be fine. Probably. She had to believe he'd be fine.

Erik cackled again, and she followed his line of sight to learn what he found so amusing. Her heart squeezed when she noticed Hari on the other side of the door's glass panels. The child sat out there, quivering with fright.

The bastard had put a spiked pinch collar around the boy's neck, with the lead connected to the balcony railing.

"Real simple, Win-Win. It's you and me and baby makes

three. Of course, you could try to fight back again, even tell me you're not going to do what I say. But I know you'll play along, because deep down inside, you'd just love it if a little boy had to watch his mother die. Again."

On the bed, Jaya stiffened and cried out, "No! Do not hurt my son."

Laughing, Erik swiveled his aim to Jaya. "I didn't say he would be hurt. I said he would have to watch you die. And Winter here is going to do it, because she's so good at that sort of thing."

… empathy and responsibility for Subject A may have been contributing psychological factors in Subject B's cooperation.

No such empathy or responsibility existed for Erik.

Winter wanted to tear his skin off in strips. She wanted to pluck out his eyes and smash them under her heel. Everything she'd been prepared for had come to pass, except instead of having the upper hand as she'd planned, she found herself trapped in a confined space, cut off from the outside world.

And facing a do-or-die choice that doesn't have a good outcome. The only way to win this is to deny him the option of forcing me to choose, and the only way to do that is to die myself.

Or kill him first.

Let's make that Plan A.

He kicked at her foot. "Hey, baby, here's how it's gonna go. You're going to kill Mommy Dearest while Harry watches. I don't really care how you do it, but I think it'd be all poetic and shit if you snapped her neck, just like you did with Timmy Bimmy's parents."

Jaya shrieked and shrank against the wall. "Winter, what is he saying?"

Her eyes stung, and Erik's ongoing cackles burned in her ears with the memory of that night at the RV park…the night her brother forced her to murder Timothy Stewart's parents in front of him.

I could've watched him die instead, and then watched as Justin killed the parents too. Or I could've tried to get the gun from him and been shot myself.

The possibilities played out in her mind, all the different ways she might've fought back against Justin, and how she might fight back against Erik now.

She saw her brother's face, pinched up with glee as he taunted her, holding the gun on Nicole Stewart first and shooting her while her mother and brother wailed and screamed in terror.

Though Subject A is the de facto authority figure in this situation...

No.

In that moment, Justin's face had gone slack. When he shot Nicole, all emotion vanished from his eyes. His mouth closed in a thin line, as if he were operating on autopilot.

That's because he wasn't in control. Douglas Kilroy was.

Kilroy had been a serial killer who'd left Winter for dead after butchering her parents. He'd kidnapped Justin that night and raised him to be his own child, mentoring him in the ways of terror and murder.

But Erik Waller wasn't raised by a serial killer. He had a parent he didn't like, a father who might've abused him or neglected him. But he hadn't been trained to become a demon in the flesh.

That meant Winter could turn the tables. She looked up at his twitching face, his eyes glassy with whatever intoxicants he'd been using to fuel his vile mania. Or maybe kill some pain. His leg looked injured, and some kind of infection appeared to be seeping through his pants.

He smiled at her.

"Ready to go steady? C'mon, show us what you're made of. Kill her." He aimed the gun at Jaya. "Or I will."

"I'm not your plaything, Erik."

He snickered. "Ha, we'll see about that. I bet we're gonna get up to all sorts of fun and games, but we have to start somewhere. You know, first date kinda stuff. I'm really looking forward to what the future holds for us, so…how about you get on with it?"

Winter wiped her face, feeling the sting and burn slowly receding. Her vision remained cloudy, but she could see that Erik had moved near the foot of the bed so he could keep all three of his hostages in view.

The gun tracked back and forth in his grip, roving from Jaya to Hari and back again. "What's it gonna be, milady? Are you going to show us what you're capable of, or do I have to do the dirty work for you?"

Two choices, both awful and both evil, were worse than no choice at all. But that was how Justin saw the world because he'd been tormented and sculpted by a mass murderer. He'd become that killer's protégé and replacement, and he'd been determined to bring Winter over to his way of thinking.

Just like Erik thought he was doing now.

Except his evil didn't have the same origin as Justin's, didn't run as deep. Instead of being made into a monster, Erik Waller was just an awful person. He might've suffered as a child, but he'd never been instructed in how to kill for pleasure or how to manipulate others and take advantage of them.

He'd had choices and chances all his life, and he'd ignored them in favor of satisfying his ego, his need for power and control. He might've been damaged, but he wasn't forced to become a monster.

He'd chosen that path himself.

"You want to be Justin, but you're nothing like him. You know that, right?"

Erik's smile wilted, and his eyes burned with fury. He thrust the gun toward Jaya. "If you want her to get dead, keep talking."

Winter smiled, knowing she'd found the crack in his armor. Outright mockery could set him off. The right amount of needling would inspire him to act on impulse, and that would be her chance to take him down. "Justin would never make threats. He would tell you what he wanted done and expect you to do it."

"I said shut your hole. I'll light up this whole damn house if I have to. Wanna watch Mommy and baby go boom?"

She couldn't see a bomb anywhere, but that didn't mean Erik was lying.

"Where's the bomb? Is it big enough to take us all down?"

He laughed. "Seriously, girl? C'mon, I know you're better than that. Hell, even your lame-ass brother knew you wouldn't take the *final* final step. He got you to do the unthinkable. Speaking of which, let's get on with your second chance at greatness."

He motioned with his other hand toward the bed. Winter moved to the left, keeping her gaze on him until she could see Jaya in her peripheral view.

"Let them go, Erik. You want me, you can have me. One on one. Just let them go."

"Ooooh," he rubbed his crotch, "I want you to say that again. Please."

Winter noticed Jaya inching toward the edge of the bed. Erik's attention was fully on Winter now, even though he'd moved his aim to Hari, who leaned against the balcony door, watching with wide eyes and tears pouring down his face.

She would play along until he moved the gun. Then she would act. "I said let them go, and you can have me. Is that what you wanted to hear?"

He smirked and stepped closer, still aiming the gun at Hari but with both eyes fixed on her. He looked her up and down and nodded. "Yeah. And you know, I think maybe the kid's going to turn out all right. Better than he would've if we'd left him in that domestic hellhole of a family."

Jaya lurched for the balcony, her mangled foot trailing a smear of blood. The door slammed open just as Erik pivoted. Two deafening cracks split the air. Her leg jerked sideways mid-step, the force spinning her onto the balcony like a ragdoll. Blood splattered the glass. Hari's screams pierced the room.

As Erik pointed his weapon, Winter launched, slamming into Erik's gut with everything she had, driving him backward. They crashed to the floor, her shoulder braced against his ribs. She clawed for the gun—fingertips brushing metal—but he twisted, snarling, and slammed it against her brow. Pain flashed white. Blood clouded her vision.

Still, she didn't let go.

He roared, hammering the gun into her back. "You're mine! I get to say what happens!" His voice cracked under the weight of rage. "Look at this. Look!"

Winter managed to roll enough to block his next strike, arm shaking as she forced his wrist down. With another cackling laugh, he reached into his pocket, his hand reappearing, this time holding a phone.

A detonator?

No. It wasn't. Instead, he swiped his thumb to reveal something more horrifying.

Gramma Beth.

On the screen, Winter's grandmother sat on her porch, with the sun's rays warming her while she sipped from a cup of tea. Potted plants framed her chair, all the shrubs and flowers that Noah had set up for her grandparents.

Why was he showing her this? What did it mean?

Erik grinned. "Gram-Gram is going to go boom-boom if you don't chill the fuck out. Now get on the bed where you belong."

32

Dazed, winded, and bloodied, Winter stayed on the floor. She retreated just enough that she could see Erik's legs move. If he tried to kick her, she'd see it coming and could intercept his foot.

"How do I know you have a bomb at their house? That could just be another camera you put up."

Erik chuckled. "Yeah, well. Could be, but it isn't." He lifted the phone and tapped at the screen, turning it around to show her.

The view had changed to her and Noah's home in Destiny Bluff. "Here comes my flowerpot party. Watch closely now."

She did, and the flowers Noah had planted on their porch began exploding, one by one. Bright flashes of light erupted with sprays of dirt and chips of terra-cotta.

His eyes flashed with glee and malice. "How old is Gram-Gram anyway? Old enough to survive a dozen flash-bangs going off all around her? What do you think'll do her in, the fright, the smoke, or maybe a stray piece of ceramic getting lodged in her eye? Pretty nasty way to go."

On the balcony, Jaya frantically pulled at the lead Erik

had wrapped around the railing. Hari cowered beneath his mother. Winter spotted a small padlock holding the collar around the boy's neck.

"Just let them go. Please. They don't deserve any of this."

"Gotta disagree with you there, Wintilicious."

His singsong voice and childlike attitude spiked rage into Winter's chest. Justin had used the same tactics to taunt and abuse her.

She stared at the gun in his hand. He moved the muzzle, first back and forth in front of her, then up and down her torso.

A slam against the door startled them both. The frame splintered and groaned, and the door pulled away on one side. Erik aimed and fired three times. Winter launched herself at him once again, knocking the phone from his hand.

She tackled him against the wall and grabbed for the gun, but he thrust his arm out and kept firing until the gun went dry. Winter slammed her palm under his chin after that, knocking his head back. He fought with an incredible intensity, slashing at her with the now-empty gun and clawing at her face with his other hand.

Winter thrust her knee up, only managing to strike the inside of his leg, though she'd been aiming for that wet wound. She tried again.

Bullseye.

As he howled in pain, the door behind her creaked and groaned. Wood splintered, and Noah shouted a warning. Erik dropped her gun and shoved her off him with both hands. He whipped a hand behind his back and came up with another pistol.

Winter caught a glimpse of Noah's face blazing with fury.

"No!" She threw herself on top of Erik again as he fired, crying out when the blazing pain of a bullet sliced across her forearm. She knocked his hand with the gun back and swung an elbow at his long, pointy nose.

Blood sprayed out, and he roared, crashing against her and attempting to bulldoze her back toward the doorway. She grabbed for the gun and twisted it free, turning the weapon on him and emptying the magazine into his chest.

With a look of surprise so comical Winter almost laughed, Erik fell back, blood pouring from his nose and oozing from the multiple holes in his body. Winter held the gun on him as Noah wrapped his arms around her from behind.

"He's dead, Winter. You stopped him."

She stayed frozen in position. "Not yet."

Erik slid down the wall, gurgling and clutching at his chest with a feeble hand as blood drained from his wounds. Thick blossoms of dark red merged together on his shirt until he sank to the floor and collapsed in an awkward pile.

She waited until his last exhale of air before throwing the gun onto the bed and turning to embrace her husband, burying her face in his collar. She clung to his shoulders before sliding her arms down to encircle him. Noah flinched away, and she felt the bandage around his hip. A dark stain spread down his leg.

"He got you. How bad is it?"

"Bad enough to remind me never to get shot again. That shit hurts."

Eve came up, holding a riot shield in one hand with impact marks on it. "Wish I'd been closer when the shooting started. Might've saved Dalton from adding to his collection of battle scars."

"I can only count to nine now too."

Without even the strength to groan at Noah's amputation joke, Winter could do nothing but watch as Eve went to the balcony door and opened it.

"Eve, please have someone go check on my grandparents. Remove them from their house until everything's clear."

Eve nodded and lifted her wrist to speak into her mic. "Done." She then turned her focus on Jaya and Hari, who were still huddled together against the railing. "You're safe now. Let's get that collar off you. Winter, check that asshole's pockets for some keys, will you?"

After kissing her husband's cheek, Winter slid from his arms and knelt by the dead man to pat his pants pockets. "Do you have any gloves on you?"

Nodding, Eve came back in, pulled a pair from her jacket, and handed them over.

Winter put them on and fished a key ring out of Erik's pocket. She passed it to Eve.

Once Hari and his mother were safely inside and the bomb squad had cleared the home of all traps, Eve directed them into the hallway.

Waiting officers from Davenport's team received them. They helped Jaya and Hari downstairs to where paramedics were ready to provide care. Winter needed to check in there, too, sooner rather than later.

That could wait.

At that moment, she wanted relief. Or satisfaction. Something. But there was only silence inside her—no celebration, no victory. Just a quiet ache in the spaces Erik had filled with fear.

She stared at his body. Not because she needed to see him dead, but because she needed to remember he'd been real. Real, and still not enough to make her into what he hoped she'd become.

He'd tried to crown himself the next monster in her life, to outdo Justin in cruelty and control. But all he'd proven was how small a man could be when he built his identity on the back of other people's pain.

Winter exhaled, slow and steady.

Hari. Jaya. Manoj. They would go home.

And she...she would live with the things she'd done. The choices she'd made. The cost of them. But she didn't regret it.

Not this time.

Because she hadn't killed for vengeance or rage or survival alone. She'd killed to stop a man who would never stop himself. She'd made a choice—an impossible one, maybe—but hers.

That part of her Justin tried to destroy? It hadn't died. It had crawled out of that trailer bloodied and screaming and still alive.

She didn't need to be clean to be good. Didn't need to be whole to be strong.

This was never about becoming someone else's version of a hero—or a monster.

This was about *legacy*. Winter's legacy. Not the one Justin tried to write for her, or the one Erik hoped to stain her with.

But the one she chose.

The one built in blood and mercy, strength and sorrow.

The one that said, *I stood between them and the dark. And I didn't back down.*

33

Winter stepped into the hospital room with a small glass vase cradled in her hands, filled with wildflowers she'd picked up from the stand outside. Simple. Bright. Alive.

In the hospital bed, Jaya opened her eyes and managed a tired smile. Her foot was wrapped tight in layers of bandages, and faint bruises colored her temples. But her eyes still held fight. Even in the aftermath, even with her body battered—she was still here.

It was beautiful to witness.

The doctors were watching her for signs of a TBI, just to be safe. Hari was with his cousins now, tucked into a safe place. He'd start therapy tomorrow. There was no shortcut around what he'd been through. But he wouldn't face it alone.

Manoj was in stable condition down the hall. Winter had stopped in to see him first. He'd given her a crooked grin and asked if she liked baseball.

After Winter set the flowers down, Jaya reached for her hand, fingers cool and trembling. "Hari is a good child." Her voice was barely audible. "He will be okay. And Manoj..." Tears filled her eyes. She couldn't finish.

She didn't need to.

"He'll be okay too." Winter squeezed her hand between both of hers. "They both will. It might take some time and help, but they'll get there. You will too. And if you need anything...a referral, a talk, someone who understands what it's like to walk through hell and come out the other side, you can call me."

Jaya's gaze lifted to hers, sharp. "Do you really believe that? Or is that just what you say to make us feel better?"

The edge in her voice didn't sting. It was honest. Desperate. Human.

Winter's mind wandered to something Autumn had said after they finally saved Timothy Stewart and put Justin away for good.

"You ended it, and now you sure as hell better start letting yourself live out those happy thoughts."

Winter often wondered how much of what she believed came from her training at Quantico and how much came from surviving encounters with humanity's monsters. "I believe what I said, Jaya, yes. Because if I don't, then I'm just giving the monsters what they've always wanted. And I can't let that happen."

"What does that mean?"

"It means we didn't survive just to keep suffering. Erik Waller doesn't get to decide who you are now. Or who I am. Or what happens next. We do. That's the only way this story ends right."

Jaya looked away, toward the window. Light filtered in through the blinds, soft and golden.

"Thank you," she said after a long silence. "For saving my sons."

Winter waited until she faced her again. "You saved them.

You never stopped fighting. You knew Manoj was in that cabin. You wrapped yourself around Hari like your body was his shield. That matters more than you know."

The tiniest of smiles lifted the corners of Jaya's lips. "I'd do anything for my boys."

"I know. When I visited Manoj, he told me how lucky he was to have you as a mother." Winter chuckled. "Right before he started talking about baseball and how he's hoping to play next season."

Jaya's smile grew a fraction wider.

"Said maybe he'll finally convince you to switch sides. Rangers to Astros."

"That boy…" Jaya yawned, her eyes growing heavy. "He asks too much."

As if they had a will of their own, Jaya's eyes finally closed. Her breaths grew slower, deeper. Rest finally winning out.

Winter eased her hand free and rose. She inhaled the fragrance of the bouquet, touched a soft flower. So soft. So pretty.

As she stepped into the hallway, a hush settled over her. Not emptiness.

Just peace.

Her legacy wasn't written in headlines or medals. It was here, in the quiet after the storm. In the lives still burning bright.

34

The last box wasn't heavy, just awkward.

Winter nudged it into the apartment with her hip, trying not to trip over Grampa Jack's newest obsession—an oversized magnifying lamp clamped to a rolling table, positioned like it was ready to perform surgery on a jigsaw puzzle.

"Don't move that!" Grampa Jack hollered from the kitchen. "I've got the edges sorted."

Gramma Beth grunted from behind the recliner. "The man's been working on this thing for six days and he's got the *edges*. Tell me again why we didn't get a smaller table?"

"Because he *needed* the one with wheels," Winter reminded her, setting the box by the couch and brushing dust from her palms.

Grampa Jack stuck his head around the corner. "It's ergonomic."

"It's enormous," Gramma Beth shot back. With a shake of her head, she turned to Winter and smiled. "Tea?"

"Yes, please."

As she poured from the pitcher, Noah stepped in behind

her, carrying a second box and sweating down the sides of his shirt. "Remind me again how they fit all this in a two-bedroom cottage?"

Gramma Beth handed him a glass of lemonade. "Love and hoarding." She batted her lashes. "Heavy on the hoarding."

Laughter bubbled up in Winter's chest. For the first time in weeks, maybe months, she let herself lean into it. The apartment was small but filled with light and that lived-in warmth only grandparents could cultivate in under thirty days.

A cross-stitch that read *Bless This Mess* hung crooked over the coat rack. Framed photos were already arranged on the sideboard—weddings, babies, old cars, and one of Grampa Jack and Gramma Beth on their honeymoon, her giving the camera a scandalized side-eye while he wore a flamingo floaty around his waist.

A knock came from the open door.

"Hellooo?" A woman sang out. "I brought scones, but I'll leave them near the door if now's a bad time."

Gramma Beth perked up. "That'll be Ginny. She lives down the hall and thinks I don't eat enough."

Grampa Jack, who'd taken a seat at his puzzle, scoffed. "She thinks I eat *too* much. Keeps bringing me diet soda like I won't notice."

Ginny swept in with a floral plate of pastries, trailing perfume and gossip. She wore a bright pink *Yes, I'm Old, But I Got to See All the Cool Bands* sweatshirt and pointed at Noah.

"You must be the newlyweds. He's cute, Beth." She winked. "Good job."

Noah crossed his arms. "Thank you?"

Ginny leaned toward Winter. "If he ever steps out of line, I know a guy who can make him disappear. Two-for-one deals if you bring a friend."

Gramma Beth snorted tea through her nose.

Grampa Jack wheezed into his puzzle.

And Winter—who'd spent her entire life building walls against pain—was overwhelmed with gratitude for this little room bursting with love and weirdness.

After Ginny swept out as quickly as she'd swept in, Winter helped herself to a scone, took Gramma Beth's hand, and led her toward the last box. "Come on. Let's do this one together."

They unpacked photos and old books and a tiny ceramic pig Gramma Beth insisted was *good luck*. When they reached the bottom, she grew quiet. Reaching into the last box, she carefully unwrapped a frame, her fingers slowing as she turned it over.

She handed it to Winter without a word.

It was a drawing, faded crayon on lined paper. Her name scrawled across the top in crooked letters. *Winter Black, Age 9.*

A whole family, drawn in blocky, colorful joy. Her mom and dad stood in the middle, arms touching. Justin, so small, grinned beside them, holding a green dinosaur that took up half his body. On the other side, Gramma Beth and Grampa Jack flanked a stick figure with wild black hair—Winter herself—each of them holding one of her hands.

The sight hit like a punch to the heart.

So much had changed.

Her parents, gone because of Douglas Kilroy's obsession. Justin…twisted by pain into something monstrous. The family in the drawing no longer existed.

But Gramma Beth and Grampa Jack were still here. Still standing. Still loving her with a fierceness that had never once wavered. Still *home*, in every way that mattered.

Winter swallowed hard and gave a small, breathless laugh. "I can't believe you still have this."

Gramma Beth ran a finger down the glass. "There's not a thing I'd rather have."

Winter didn't speak. Couldn't. She just set the frame on the shelf beside Gramma Beth's favorite books and let it settle there—like a memory, like a monument, like a promise.

A reminder of what was lost.

And everything she still had.

Gramma Beth turned to Winter, her expression soft but steady. "You've carried the weight of the world for so long, dearie. It's okay to set it down."

Winter nodded, throat tight.

Gramma Beth squeezed her hand. "You're not just meant to fight monsters, you know. You're meant to live too."

Winter blinked back tears. "I think I'm ready to try."

Later, as the sun dipped low and a few more new friends stopped by her grandparents' cozy apartment, Winter stepped back and watched them hold court—laughing, storytelling, slipping into this next chapter of life with grace and ease. They were exactly where they were meant to be.

Noah came up behind her, his warmth pressing into her spine as he wrapped his arms around her. She leaned into him, grounding herself in the solidness of his presence.

She had her family. Her love. Her peace.

She had a future worth running toward.

The monsters would come again, someday.

But for now—for today—the light was winning.

35

The sea at Cinque Terre didn't crash. It whispered.

Winter sat curled on a cushioned bench just beyond their villa's terrace, mug of rich Italian coffee warming her hands. Below, the waves lapped at the shore with slow, patient rhythm, the kind that made you forget time even existed.

Noah joined her, blanket draped over his shoulders like a cape, his tablet in one hand and a chocolate croissant in the other.

"Guess who's emailing me at six in the morning?"

Winter didn't even need to look at the screen. "Falkner?"

"Got it in one." He raised his brows and read aloud. "'Any chance you'd consider consulting earlier than planned? The Chicago division is asking if you're available.'"

Winter gave him a sideways look.

Noah smirked and started typing. "Respectfully, sir, my wife and I are currently on a three-week, no-suitcases-needed vacation in paradise. I'll be back after that. Until then, we're off the clock."

Winter clapped, even though a small part of her—maybe

the same one that used to sleep with her phone under her pillow—felt a flicker of curiosity about the case. But it could wait.

He hit Send with a flourish and tossed the tablet onto the cushion beside him. "There. First boundary of our marriage, clearly stated."

Winter laughed and leaned her head on his shoulder. "Well done, Agent Dalton."

He kissed the top of her head. "Detective Black-Dalton, you're welcome."

They sat in comfortable silence for a while, watching light spill across the horizon like gold silk. The tablet pinged, and Noah reached for the device again.

Winter groaned. "Really?"

"Just turning the damn thing on mute…oh." Noah tapped the screen. "Another message from Falkner, but not about work this time. They finally tracked down the guard who helped Justin stay in touch with the outside world. He's in custody, and he's talking. Said Justin manipulated him into thinking he was part of something…righteous."

Winter closed her eyes. Not from pain, not anymore. Just a sense of closure finally landing with both feet.

"It's really over."

Noah set the tablet aside again and shifted, wrapping an arm around her. "It's over."

She reached for his hands, pulling them gently into her lap. Her thumb brushed over the inked ring permanently etched at the base of what was left of his fourth finger—the finger Erik had taken in a twisted attempt to break her.

He'd tattooed the stump a week ago, there in Italy. A ring he could never lose. A symbol that defied the violence meant to destroy them.

Her fingers moved to his right wrist, where a faint scar

still lingered—the ghost of the handcuffs she'd slapped on him during the chaos of the case.

"Still can't believe you let me cuff you to the wheel." She knew she was opening a can of very sensitive worms but couldn't help herself.

Noah grinned, eyes dancing. "You say *let* like I had a choice."

She laughed and turned to straddle his thighs. "You were being *very* dramatic."

His eyes narrowed. "I was handcuffed. In the middle of a crime scene. That's not drama. That's trauma."

She kissed the side of his jaw. "It was also necessary."

He nuzzled her neck, his tone dipping into mischief. "Next time you cuff me, maybe have the decency to follow through."

Her laugh startled a few birds from a nearby tree. "Are you saying you're into that now?"

"I'm saying I was left alone in a car with my own thoughts and zero snacks. It was traumatizing."

She rolled her eyes and ran a finger down his chest. "I'll pack snacks next time."

"Promise?"

"Maybe."

She let the moment hang, gentle and real.

"You ever think about what's next for us?"

He ran fingers through her hair, his eyes softening. "All the time."

The weight of everything they'd survived seemed to melt under that quiet admission. Winter rose to her feet, tugging on his hand. "Come on."

Noah followed without question, his smile both wicked and wide. "Back to bed?" The amount of hope in his voice could have filled a million balloons.

She leaned in close. "We might need more practice."

He didn't wait to be asked twice.

They disappeared into the villa, the sun climbing behind them, a new day unfolding.

Winter had spent her life standing between the innocent and the monsters.

But now?

Now she got to stand in the light.

And when they returned—refreshed, recharged, more in love than ever—there'd be work waiting.

Darnell Davenport had made sure of that, championing Winter's Distinguished Service Citation from the chief of police. It came with the kind of quiet respect that opened old case files, gave her unofficial authority, and let her do what she did best…help.

Ariel was holding down the fort in the meantime, handling paperwork, reviewing cold cases Darnell sent over, and screening prospective clients. No fieldwork. Not yet. Just the structure. The system. The groundwork.

And maybe the best news of all? The FBI had officially signed off on their partnership with Black Investigations.

The future wasn't something they feared anymore.

It was something they got to build—together.

And hopefully soon, their love would grow into something more—a life shaped by peace, not fear.

> *You've seen me at my worst. My most broken.*
> *You stayed through the darkest moments*
> *Now you get to leave me in the light.*
> *And I can't think of a better ending than that.*
> *Love always,*
> *Winter.*

The End.

Thank you for reading.
All of the Winter Black Series books can be found on Amazon.

NOTE FROM THE AUTHOR

I've written many characters, but none have stayed with me the way Winter Black has. She started as a spark—just a whisper of a woman with a gun and a haunted past. But across so many books covering two full seasons, she became something else entirely. She became family.

Writing this final installment was one of the hardest things I've ever done. Not because I didn't know how it should end—but because I didn't want to say goodbye. Winter's strength, her fury, her relentless pursuit of justice…they've inspired me more than I can ever express.

To the readers who took this journey with her—thank you. You cried with her, fought beside her, and never stopped believing in her. She was never just a character. She was *ours*.

And to the incredible team who helped bring her to life—my editors, my early readers, and everyone behind the scenes—

thank you for helping me shape her story into one I'll always be proud of.

I'll miss and love her forever. But what a ride it's been.

And knowing that she's found peace at last—and that I can revisit her story any time I open a book—makes saying goodbye just a little bit easier.

ACKNOWLEDGMENTS

The past few years have been a whirlwind of change, both personally and professionally, and I find myself at a loss for the right words to express my profound gratitude to those who have supported me on this remarkable journey. Yet, I am compelled to try.

To my sons, whose unwavering support has been my bedrock, granting me the time and energy to transform my darkest thoughts into words on paper. Your steadfast belief in me has never faltered, and watching each of you grow, welcoming the wonderful daughters you've brought into our family, has been a source of immense pride and joy.

Embarking on the dual role of both author and publisher has been an exhilarating, albeit challenging, adventure. Transitioning from the solitude of writing to the dynamic world of publishing has opened new horizons for me, and I'm deeply grateful for the opportunity to share my work directly with you, the readers.

I extend my heartfelt thanks to the entire team at Mary Stone Publishing, the same dedicated group who first recognized my potential as an indie author years ago. Your collective efforts, from the editors whose skillful hands have polished my words to the designers, marketers, and support staff who breathe life into these books, have been instrumental in resonating deeply with our readers. Each of you plays a crucial role in this journey, not only nurturing my growth but also ensuring that every story reaches its full potential. Your dedication, creativity, and finesse have been nothing short of invaluable.

However, my deepest gratitude is reserved for you, my beloved readers. You ventured off the beaten path of traditional publishing to embrace my work, investing your most precious asset—your time. It is my sincerest hope that this book has enriched that time, leaving you with memories that linger long after the last page is turned.

With all my love and heartfelt appreciation,

Mary

ABOUT THE AUTHOR

Nestled in the serene Blue Ridge Mountains of East Tennessee, Mary Stone crafts her stories surrounded by the natural beauty that inspires her. What was once a home filled with the lively energy of her sons has now become a peaceful writer's retreat, shared with cherished pets and the vivid characters of her imagination.

As her sons grew and welcomed wonderful daughters-in-law into the family, Mary's life entered a quieter phase, rich with opportunities for deep creative focus. In this tranquil environment, she weaves tales of courage, resilience, and intrigue, each story a testament to her evolving journey as a writer.

From childhood fears of shadowy figures under the bed to a profound understanding of humanity's real-life villains, Mary's style has been shaped by the realization that the most complex antagonists often hide in plain sight. Her writing is characterized by strong, multifaceted heroines who defy traditional roles, standing as equals among their peers in a world of suspense and danger.

Mary's career has blossomed from being a solitary author to establishing her own publishing house—a significant milestone that marks her growth in the literary world. This expansion is not just a personal achievement but a reflection of her commitment to bring thrilling and thought-provoking stories to a wider audience. As an author and publisher, Mary continues to challenge the conventions of the thriller genre, inviting readers into gripping tales filled with serial killers, astute FBI agents, and intrepid heroines who confront peril with unflinching bravery.

Each new story from Mary's pen—or her publishing house—is a pledge to captivate, thrill, and inspire, continuing the legacy of the imaginative little girl who once found wonder and mystery in the shadows.

Discover more about Mary Stone on her website.
www.authormarystone.com

facebook.com/authormarystone
x.com/MaryStoneAuthor
goodreads.com/AuthorMaryStone
bookbub.com/authors/mary-stone
instagram.com/marystoneauthor

Printed in Great Britain
by Amazon